"Mommy!" A miniature blond whirlwind appeared on the step.

Mommy? Dallas blinked as his wife grasped one tiny hand and led the child to stand in front of him.

"I want you to meet someone, Misty," Gracie said. "This is Dallas. He's your daddy."

"My daddy?" The tiny girl wearing a mussed blue dress touched his knee, and in doing so, grabbed hold of Dallas's heart.

His daughter.

She was an immature version of her mom. Feathery, golden curls spilled to her shoulders. Perfect features in a sun-kissed face.

But Misty wasn't all Gracie. The jut of her chin, the dimple that flickered at the edge of her mouth—he knew those were his gifts to her. He'd studied his own features in the mirror so often, trying to remember who he was.

He was a father.

Books by Lois Richer

Love Inspired

A Will and a Wedding #8
*Faithfully Yours #15
*A Hopeful Heart #23
*Sweet Charity #32
A Home, a Heart,
    a Husband #50
This Child of Mine #59
**Baby on the Way #73
**Daddy on the Way #79
**Wedding on the Way #85
‡Mother's Day Miracle #101
‡His Answered Prayer #115

‡Blessed Baby #152
Tucker's Bride #182
Inner Harbor #207
†Blessings #226
†Heaven's Kiss #237
†A Time to Remember #256
Past Secrets, Present Love #328
‡‡His Winter Rose #385
‡‡Apple Blossom Bride #389
‡‡Spring Flowers,
    Summer Love #392
§Healing Tides #432
§Heart's Haven #435
§A Cowboy's Honor #441

Love Inspired Suspense

A Time To Protect #13
††Secrets of the Rose #27
††Silent Enemy #29
††Identity: Undercover #31

*Faith, Hope & Charity
**Brides of the Season
‡If Wishes Were Weddings
†Blessings in Disguise
††Finders Inc.
‡‡Serenity Bay
§Pennies from Heaven

LOIS RICHER

likes variety. From her time in human resources management to entrepreneurship, life has held plenty of surprises.

"Having given up on fairy tales, I was happily involved in building a restaurant when a handsome prince walked into my life and upset all my career plans with a wedding ring. Motherhood quickly followed. I guess the seeds of my storytelling took root because of two small boys who kept demanding, "Then what, Mom?"

The miracle of God's love for His children, the blessing of true love, the joy of sharing Him with others—that is a story that can be told a thousand ways and yet still be brand-new. Lois Richer intends to go right on telling it.

A Cowboy's Honor
Lois Richer

Steeple
Hill®

Published by Steeple Hill Books™

STEEPLE HILL BOOKS

Steeple
Hill®

ISBN-13: 978-0-373-87477-4
ISBN-10:   0-373-87477-4

A COWBOY'S HONOR

...And we confidently and joyfully look forward to becoming all that He has had in mind for us to be.

—*Romans* 5:2b

Chapter One

Hope was a wasted effort, thought Gracie Henderson as she walked through the park at the Dallas Arboretum. There on a hillock she found the spot she remembered dearly, where she'd first met her cowboy. Now, staring at the exact spot where he'd entered her life, she noticed a man hunched down in the grass. Birds gathered around him, swooping down from the sky. They landed on toothpick legs, then moved toward him in tiny stops and starts.

Intrigued, Gracie paused to watch.

The man's face was turned away from her, but something about the way he sat, something in his frozen stillness would not let her look away.

He pulled off a morsel of whatever was in his hand with exaggerated slowness. Without so much as a muscle twitch he held it out, wordlessly coaxing the birds nearer until they lit upon his hand and pecked the food from his fingers. Entranced children flocked near the bird man, trying to emulate his success with the feathered animals as their bemused families watched.

Gracie blinked, checked her watch. Not a lot of time to spare. Since the wrought-iron bench she sought out was unoccupied, she sat down, but left her lunch bag unopened. In this particular place, in the warm rays of the May sun, her aching soul felt soothing relief.

Gracie had been back in Texas only a week, but that was long enough to dull her memories of the cooler North Dakota spring she'd left behind. It was almost long enough for Dallas's southern heat to evaporate the chill encasing her heart.

For the next six months they would be safe.

She pressed her back against the warm metal and soaked in the lake view, breathed the heady scents of blooming alyssum and freshly mowed grass, listened to the breeze rustle the lush leaves of a nearby cottonwood. All of it combined sent her thoughts headlong into the past, into emotions she'd struggled to bury.

She'd been so happy that day, so trusting.

Reality splashed down like a cold shower, reminding her that her blissful joy had lasted eight short days. At least she'd learned from that. Now she took precautions, made sure before she leaped.

With effort Gracie pushed away the hurt and opened her lunch bag. From the corner of her eye she noticed the man rise. He ambled across the grass, pausing to sniff at a bed of flowers, then pluck a tumbled leaf from the grass.

Gracie bit into her chicken salad sandwich and closed her eyes, allowing herself a moment to savor her lunch. Simple joys. She'd learned not to take them for granted.

"It's a beautiful place, isn't it?"

Gracie blinked, stared at the owner of that butter-smooth voice.

Her heart stopped.

He looked so real standing in front of her, watching her with a quizzical stare. Nothing at all like the man in her dreams. Her cowboy.

"Dallas?" she squeaked. Gracie's heart beat in a painful rhythm, and she grasped the edge of the bench for support.

"It's a pretty city, but I didn't know it would be so hot." He swiped a hand across his forehead, smiled. A familiar dimple peeked out from the corner of his mouth. "And this is only spring."

How she'd missed those bittersweet eyes.

"You've chosen the prettiest spot. Do you mind if I share it?"

Gracie shook her head. Her limbs trembled with excitement until terror, cold as Arctic ice, grabbed hold, plunging her from delight to dread in two seconds flat. Something was wrong.

She didn't know what to ask first.

Dallas didn't try to break the silence between them. In fact, he seemed to relish it. A faint smile curved his lips as a bird flitted closer to beg for food.

It was a mirage, a dream. It had to be. Only Gracie couldn't wake up.

So many times, through long sleepless nights and terror-filled days, she'd longed to share her burden, to talk to him, to lean against his shoulder and know she wasn't alone, that she didn't have to be afraid anymore.

After the first year alone, filled with questions that were never answered, she'd shoved him out of her mind and never permitted herself to imagine him coming back.

Now here he was.

"Where have you been, Dallas?" Rage replaced curiosity. "Did you even consider how worried I was? Surely you could have called, written—something?"

Terror filled his face. He was afraid? Of her?

He jumped up from the grass.

"I didn't mean to bother you, ma'am. I'm sorry I…"

Brown eyes brimmed with shadows she didn't understand. But his fear was obvious. A riot of emotions flashed in his eyes, a wariness she'd never expected. As if she were a stranger.

Gracie stood up in turn, touched his arm. "Don't you think you owe me some kind of explanation, Dallas?"

He fidgeted as if he found her touch painful. Then he grew still and his eyes met hers for the first time.

Empty eyes.

"You…know me?"

She might have missed his question if she hadn't been standing inches away.

"Of course I know you." Anger chased frustration. "What are you playing at, Dallas?"

His Adam's apple bobbed as he struggled to swallow. "So my name is Dallas."

Gracie pulled back. This was not the man she knew. This was a stranger in his body—a wary stranger who showed no signs of recognizing her. She longed to shake him, to finally pry loose the responses she'd been denied. But his uncertainty, the watchful way he peeked at her, like one of those wary birds he'd been feeding… Gracie gulped down her bitterness, sought nonchalance.

"What's been going on with you, Dallas?"

"Dallas what?" He stared into space, looking for all the world as if he hadn't heard the most important question she'd ever asked.

"Pardon?"

"My last name. What is it?"

"Henderson."

He turned his focus on her then, obviously mulling over something in his mind. After a moment he stepped back.

Gracie waited for an apology, an explanation. Something. But he continued to regard her with that blank stare.

"Who am I?"

His rushed whisper sounded deadly serious. But Gracie couldn't quite believe it. And until she figured out if he was playing some kind of game, she had to be cautious.

"Let's sit down on the bench. You can share my lunch. Please?" she added when it looked as if he'd refuse. "Are you hungry?"

"Not really."

"Well, I am. Maybe you could wait while I eat my lunch." Gracie drew him toward the bench, motioned for him to sit. She needed to buy some time, figure out what to do next. "I have some juice and some coffee. Which would you like?"

"I love coffee."

He always had.

She handed it over. Dallas removed the lid, sniffed and closed his eyes as he savored the aroma. The familiar gesture brought tears, but Gracie dashed them away.

She would not weep. Not then. Not now.

Not ever.

"This is good coffee. Thank you, ma'am."

If he had a hat she knew he would have doffed it. Like a gallant cowboy. Her cowboy. The sting pierced deep and hard, but Gracie was used to pain. She ignored it, focused on getting the answers she craved.

"Can you tell me where you've been?" For now she had to push back the raging inner voice and try to figure out her next move.

"California."

"What did you do there?"

"I worked with animals."

That made sense to Gracie. It didn't matter why he'd been there. She knew it would have to do with the almost spiritual rapport Dallas had always shared with animals. But that was the only part of Dallas she recognized.

"Did you come to this city straight from California?"

He nodded, accepted the half sandwich she held out, munched on it before speaking. "Yes. I needed to figure out the dream."

"You had a dream?"

He looked around. "Maybe more of a memory. Of this park, I think. It was different, but it was the same day as today. May 1." He glanced around, frowned. "I kept hearing a word. *Dallas.* So I came to Dallas." He pulled on his earlobe, fiddled with a shirt button. "I know that sounds weird."

The significance of the date may have escaped him, but Gracie couldn't forget.

"My name is Dallas. Dallas Henderson," he repeated.

She held her breath as she gently probed. "You say you couldn't remember your name before?"

"It was on the tip of my tongue, but I couldn't catch it. Do you know how that is?" He held out a bit of crust from his sandwich. The big, generous smile she remembered so well flashed when a bird hopped onto his knee and took the bread.

"Dallas, do you know my name?"

The smile vanished when he turned sideways to study her. "No."

"My name is Gracie."

"Hello, Gracie." He held out a hand, shook hers with solemn formality. "Pleased to meet you. You're very lovely. Your eyes are the color of bluebells."

"Thank you." She detected no sign of recognition on his face. For now she'd have to assume he wasn't pretending. Her heart jerked.

"Do you know me well?" Dallas played with his pant leg while he waited for her answer.

"I thought I did."

"Oh." He lifted his head, searched her face. "How did we know each other?"

"We met in this park." Gracie wasn't sure how much to reveal. "Over there. Where you were feeding the birds. On that hillock. I was here on a vacation during college."

"So I came back to a familiar place." He nodded, his brown eyes pensive. "The doctors said I might."

Doctors… So he'd been in hospital?

"Do you remember anything about being here before? About me?"

"Nothing is clear." His rubbed his temple, his visible agitation warning her to proceed with caution. "If I could only—"

"It doesn't matter." Concerned about the white pinch of his lips, she pushed back her own gnawing uncertainties. "We don't have to talk about it now."

"You're the first person I've met who knows me. I *want* to talk, to figure things out," he said, his voice slightly hoarse. "I just don't know what to talk about. I—I'm afraid."

Yes, she'd seen fear crawl into his dark eyes a few moments ago. She just hadn't recognized it. Dallas had never been afraid. Of anything.

"What is it you're afraid of?"

"There must be a reason I can't remember. Maybe I don't want to. Maybe I committed a crime, ran away from the law or something." He kept his head bent. "Maybe I was in jail and I don't want to go back."

It was so preposterous Gracie almost laughed—until she saw his hand shake as he brushed away some crumbs.

"I knew you very well, Dallas, and I'm fairly certain you were never in jail. You don't have to worry about that."

"Then why don't I remember anything?"

"I'm sure you will. Don't worry, you'll think of plenty of things to talk about in a while. Didn't the doctors say not to try too hard?"

He scanned the park once more before his gaze came to rest on her. "You know, I wasn't sure why I kept dreaming the word *Dallas* but it seemed like God was leading me to this city. This is only my second day here but it feels right. Not like California did. I didn't belong there."

God led him here? Or had chance?

Gracie preferred to think God hadn't deliberately done this to her.

Having found a subject, Dallas seemed inclined to talk. "Yesterday I looked at some maps in the library. I saw White Rock Lake and an article about the arboretum. It sounds silly, but they both seemed familiar. So I decided to see for myself. But when I got here, I couldn't remember anything more. Everything is a big blank."

"Are you staying nearby?"

"At a small motel not far away. And there's a diner near it. It's okay."

She handed him one of her cookies, mostly to buy time to think.

So Dallas was back—a different Dallas. One who had no knowledge of their past. It was unbelievable, something she'd never anticipated.

"When you knew me..." He spoke haltingly, as if still fearful of the answers his questions might bring. "What did I do? For a job, I mean."

"You're an animal behavior specialist," Gracie told him. That part was easy. "When I knew you, you had almost finished a contract working for a multinational company, traveling a lot to complete a research project. You talked about training horses after that. For police patrols, in New York, maybe? I'm not sure. You spoke of a number of different options, but they always included horses."

"Hey, maybe I was a cowboy." He grinned.

You were. My cowboy.

You were supposed to come home.

Dallas crumbled the rest of the cookie, held his outstretched hand on the bench and waited. After a moment another bird approached, and before many minutes had elapsed, it was eating from his hand.

"Do you know where I used to live in the city?"

"Actually, when I knew you, you had a place in Houston when you came back from traveling. I think your company owned it." Gracie hesitated to tell him more, her fear crowding out the joy she'd begun to allow.

This was not the Dallas she'd known. This man was a stranger. Every sense warned her to be careful about what she told him. Thankfully, she wasn't the same naive woman she'd once been.

Things had changed.

Don't forget the past. To relax her guard now could cost her everything.

"Please tell me what you know," he begged, withdrawing his hand so quickly the bird hopped backward, chattering angrily. "Please."

When she didn't speak Dallas bent forward, holding her gaze with his own. "I want to go home," he begged. "I've been away so long. Please tell me where I belong."

The ache underlying those words was Gracie's undoing.

"You belong to me," she whispered. "I'm your wife. We were married in this park six years ago today. May 1."

For what seemed eternity Dallas said nothing, simply stared at her with an intensity that made her catch her breath. Then he reached up, cupped her chin in his palm as if he couldn't help himself.

The action was so Dallas, Gracie had to blink back tears.

"I have a wife." He might have said, *I'm not alone,* so great was the relief in his voice. "I am a married man."

Gracie glanced at his left hand. Her stomach clenched. His ring finger was bare, missing the plain gold band she'd slid on it six years ago.

"Do we live nearby, Gracie?"

"No."

Though she struggled to find a balance between his need to know and her need to feel safe, Gracie couldn't deny this man was her husband. The green-gold eyes that had once melted with love for her, the hazel irises that deepened to a rich forest shade when he was serious, but lit up like Pharaoh's gold when he laughed— they were the same.

His hair was longer now, shaggy and unruly, matching his rumpled clothing and generally disheveled state. There were a few silver strands among the dark, just above his ears. He was thinner than he'd been, his jeans loose on the lean body he'd once kept in shape by jogging. Sunken cheeks and haunted eyes told her he'd survived some trauma.

But underneath he was still Dallas, still her husband.

And she knew nothing of how he'd spent the past six years.

"Where do we live?"

She could tell him that. It didn't matter now.

"We used to live in North Dakota in a little town called Turtleford. I'm a vet. My father had a practice there. I worked with him while you traveled for your business."

"The house where we lived—was it a big kind of farmhouse with dormers and a high peaked roof?"

She nodded, surprised by the description.

"I dreamed about it," he said, eyes wide. "And a purple bedroom."

Gracie smiled and nodded.

"You claimed the bedspread and drapes looked less intense in the store where you bought them."

I loved them because you gave them to me. I loved you.

Pain sliced through Gracie's heart.

"I haven't seen you in six years, Dallas. You left on a business trip out west, to Washington, and I never heard from you again. Do you have any idea why?"

She couldn't have stopped the question even if she'd wanted to. It had lain unanswered in her mind for too long. Now desperation demanded to know how the man who'd professed to love her more than life could walk away from everything they'd promised each other.

"I'm sorry." His gaze roved the park, returned to her, dazed and confused. "I don't know anything except that about three months ago I woke up in a hospital in California. They said I'd been in a coma for almost six years. I had no identification, no money. Ever since then I've been trying to figure out who I am."

Gracie's heart cracked.

"I *felt* like there was somebody I belonged to, someone who knew about my past, but I couldn't figure out whom. I guess I was thinking of you."

A smile pushed up the corners of his mouth but was quickly replaced by a frown of confusion.

"What?" she asked. A hospital… Was he in pain?

"The police put out news alerts and posters, someone set up a tip line, but no one ever called to ask about me. My dreams were the only thing I had to go on." He glanced around. "Do I have any family?"

I'm your family, a voice inside her screamed. And then a second terrifying thought took over.

His parents.

Stark, cold dread crawled up Gracie's spine and seized the cords at the back of her neck. Her throat slammed shut, choking off her air supply. Her fingers squeezed together.

Don't give in to it. Not yet.

They were his parents. They had a right to know Dallas was alive, even if he couldn't remember who they were. But that didn't mean she had to be there.

"When I got here I realized I knew my way around." He continued speaking as if nothing had changed.

And for him it hadn't.

"I didn't get lost, I didn't get confused. You said we met here." He studied her intently. "I think I know this city."

Gracie nodded. "Actually, you grew up in Dallas," she said. "Your parents live here."

"Parents?" His forehead wrinkled. "I don't remember. Any siblings?"

"No."

"Where do my parents live? Can you take me to see them?"

Gracie controlled her breathing. "I don't know if your parents live in the same place they did when we were married, Dallas. I just moved back here. We… haven't kept in touch."

He studied her quizzically, opened his mouth as if to ask why, then closed it.

Gracie blinked, marveled that the world still looked the same. But nothing would ever be the same, and she had to prepare for that.

"Grace—no, Gracie, isn't it?"

"Gracie." She blinked, pulling herself back to reality. "Yes."

"Gracie. Right." Dallas inhaled. He wrapped his hands around his knee and squeezed so hard his fingertips turned white. "Would you be able to drive me to my parents' house? I'd like to see them. Maybe then I could remember."

It was the last thing Gracie wanted to do. Her very soul rebelled. But she could hardly refuse. He was still her husband, he was alone and he was obviously troubled.

She glanced at her watch, battled to do the right thing.

"I can drop you there," she agreed finally. "But I won't be able to stay. I'm supposed to be back at the ranch by four." Her conscience pricked but she ignored it, began gathering up the remains of their lunch.

"The ranch?"

"The Bar None. It's a ranch for disabled children. I'm working there for the next six months." She wasn't going to tell him more. Not yet.

Not until she had to.

"But you said you had a practice with your father."

"No, I said I worked with him six years ago. He died." The punch of loss had weakened after all this time. "I had to sell his practice."

"Oh." Dallas waited.

Gracie refused to say more, declined to relive those black days now. Maybe in the future she could drag out all that had passed, but even then she wasn't sure she could explain without demanding to know why Dallas hadn't been there to help her survive.

"I'm parked over here." She pointed, stepped forward, then paused. "Do you have any belongings we need to pick up from your hotel?"

Dallas turned so she could see a small backpack. "Everything I own is in this."

"Okay, then. Let's go." Gracie hurried away from her favorite spot, pausing briefly to toss out the lunch she hadn't been able to finish. As anniversaries went, this one would at least be memorable.

Once inside the truck Dallas automatically fastened his seat belt. He'd always been careful to do that, said he'd seen too many accidents in his travels.

Was that what had happened to him? An accident?

"You don't look like a veterinarian."

"What do vets look like?" she countered.

He'd said nearly the same thing the first time she'd met him in this park during her college spring break. She hadn't been a vet then, only a trainee, but she'd yearned, dreamed of being more. Eventually, she'd poured out all those hopes and fears to Dallas, as he shared his with her. By Christmas they were secretly engaged.

"I guess I thought a vet would look sort of horsey." He tilted his head to one side, studied her. "You look more like a kindergarten teacher. Or a mother."

Gracie clenched the steering wheel, her palms damp.

"What did I say? Something bad? Are you okay?" Dallas examined her too closely.

She could only imagine how hard it must be to tiptoe around, trying not to offend, without really knowing the another person. No wonder he'd been afraid. Dallas had nothing to guide him.

"I'm fine." She faked a smile. "Just the traffic. It's, ah…been a while since I've driven this way."

It's been six years since I drove to your parents' home, but I remember every corner, every signpost. Her head hammered in time to the engine's sputter.

"It's pretty weird—I can't even remember my own wedding. I can see you as a bride, though. All in white, wearing one of those fluffy bridal dresses, like a ballerina." He met her glance and a hot wire of emotion singed Gracie's heart. She focused on the street ahead.

They were getting close. Too close.

"Is that what you wore, Gracie?" Dallas prodded.

"What? A ballerina dress?" She shook her head. "White cotton sundress and sandals. Nothing fancy. Couldn't afford it. You and I eloped, got married by the J.P., then came to the park." Where they'd held their own private ceremony, promising never to stop loving each other.

Had Dallas honored that promise?

"What did I wear at our wedding?" he asked several moments later.

"What you always wear—wore. Cowboy boots, black pants, white shirt and a Stetson."

Dallas stared at his sneakered feet in disbelief. "I used to wear cowboy boots?"

Though her arms ached from gripping the wheel so hard, Gracie couldn't help her smile. "I don't think I ever saw you in anything else."

"It seems like you're talking about someone I don't know. A person I've never met."

She didn't respond, was too busy quashing the fear spreading like a virus through her.

"This is it."

Gracie drew up to the curb, shoved the gearshift home and flicked off the engine. She forced air into her lungs, the metal taste of fear coating her tongue.

"This is what?"

"This was your parents' house six years ago."

"I lived here?" Dallas surveyed the big colonial with its massive lawns.

Gracie gulped, nodded. The place had changed. The abundance of flowers was gone, but perhaps his parents had grown weary of their gardening hobby. The shutters and trim had been painted recently, and were now a vivid green instead of the stark glossy black she'd remembered.

Dallas pushed his door open. He glanced over one shoulder expectantly. Only his quick breath gave away his jitters.

"Aren't you coming?"

Gracie shook her head. "I'll wait here till they let you in. Just to be sure everything's okay. Then I've got to get back to the ranch. The Bar None. You can call me there whenever you want."

They'd rejected her once. They wouldn't get a second chance.

"Go ahead, Dallas. I promise I'll wait till you're inside."

His frown testified that he wasn't pleased, but he didn't argue. He nodded once, vaulted from the truck and strode across the lawn.

Gracie swallowed a jagged little pill of fear as the familiar stride carried him so easily to the house where her dreams had crashed and burned.

Why, God? Why now, when I've just begun to put the pieces back together? Why not five years ago, when I needed him so badly?

The question died unanswered as Dallas rang the doorbell. Gracie held her breath when the big front door opened. But instead of embracing him and pulling him inside, the woman behind the screen shook her head and kept talking. Eventually she closed the door.

Dallas ambled slowly back toward the truck, his expression perplexed.

Fear's stranglehold relaxed.

Safe. Could it be that simple?

"What's wrong?" Gracie pressed back against her seat, preparing herself.

"The Hendersons, my parents, moved about four years ago. She didn't know where they moved to, only that they sold the house and talked of leaving the country." He climbed into the cab of the truck, his eyes tormented. "She thought they mentioned India."

So they were out of her life. But if Gracie found a way to contact them, to tell them Dallas was back, they'd return and nothing would be safe.

And if she didn't… Dallas stared down at his fingers, his posture showing defeat. That's when compassion pushed aside fear.

She was his wife. She had to do something.

It was risky. With no memory and no viable means of support, Dallas wasn't a threat.

Not yet.

But later on…

"We'll figure something out," she promised. "But right now you'd better come with me to the ranch." She started the engine. An emotion, quickly hidden, flickered over his face. "What's wrong?"

"You don't really want me to go with you. Why is that?" Dallas's intuition was as bang on as it always had been. His skin paled. "Did I do something wrong when we were married? Hurt you somehow?"

"Don't be silly. Of course not!"

"The way you looked at me a moment ago…I must have done something to warrant that." Dallas quietly gathered up his backpack and reached for the door handle. "Thank you for the ride, but I don't want to disrupt your life, Gracie. I'll go back to the motel for tonight. It's the New Sunrise. You can reach me there, or stop by the park. If I need you, I'll call the Bar None."

She visualized him wandering lost and alone, aimlessly feeding the birds while he waited for someone to acknowledge him, to tell him who he was, where he belonged.

"Get in and close the door, Dallas. We can sort through everything at the ranch." Her cheeks scorched with shame. "You feel lost, but remember, this is quite a shock for me. I'm struggling to absorb it all, too. But I really don't want you to go back to that motel. Not yet."

"You're sure?"

She should be ecstatic. Her husband, the man she'd loved so desperately, was home. Even better, his parents were nowhere in sight. She was safe. But none of it felt real.

"I'm sure, Dallas." She wasn't sure at all. But Gracie had no choice. "Given your way with animals, you'll fit right in. You might even hire on. They're shorthanded at the moment, and the summer kids will be arriving soon."

"You don't owe me anything, Gracie. You've gone on with your life. That's good." He patted her hand. "I don't want to impose on anyone. I only want to figure out who I am. It's really okay. I'll be fine."

Gracie reared back at his touch. Emotion could not rule her life a second time. But her skin wouldn't forget him.

"I know I haven't been very welcoming. It's just… the surprise." How lame. "I'll help you, I promise, Dallas."

They'd both promised so many things.

To love.

To honor.

In sickness and in health.

How could she have known when she made those promises that they would cost her everything?

Chapter Two

Dallas didn't like it, but his wife was his only key to figuring out his past.

He hesitated, but finally nodded. "All right, Gracie. I'll go with you, for now. Maybe there's something I can do to earn my keep." An idea formed. "If you had some photos or something that I could look at, it might help trigger my memory."

It was doubtful anything would, not after so many blank months. But he wouldn't stop hoping. Or trusting God to get him through this, however long it took.

"Sure. No problem." Gracie waited for him to buckle up.

"I'll try not to cause problems for you." As if he wasn't already. He winced. "I don't suppose it will be easy to explain my sudden appearance to anyone."

"Elizabeth won't mind."

"Elizabeth?"

"Elizabeth Wisdom. She owns the Bar None. At least her foundation does. Along with a whole lot of other places around the world."

"You work for this foundation?"

"Yes." Gracie's fingertips squeezed the steering wheel and she heaved a sigh of relief, as if she was glad of the change in subject. She had beautiful hands. They matched the rest of her. Any man would be proud to call her his wife. Which made Dallas wonder why he'd left, and where he would stay once they arrived at the ranch.

"Tell me how you came to be there."

"It was rough after my dad died," Gracie began quietly. "I hadn't finished vet school, so I wasn't qualified to take over from him. The house went with the practice. Once they were sold I didn't have anyplace to go."

His fault. Why hadn't he provided a home for his wife?

"Things got pretty bad," she summarized, casting him a sideways glance. "Elizabeth offered me a scholarship to finish my degree, with the condition that I work for the foundation for six months when I graduated."

"So you'll only be at the ranch for six months? Then where will you go?"

"I haven't figured that out yet."

Gracie flicked on the radio, leaned back and hummed along to the country-and-western song filling the cab. Whatever other questions he had would have to wait.

Such as how he came to be married to a woman who was lovelier than Hollywood's hottest celebrity, yet couldn't recall one single thing about it.

When big wrought-iron gates and a sign announcing the Bar None appeared, Dallas reached out and turned off the radio. Gracie shot him a quick glance.

"We're almost there, aren't we?"

"Yes."

"Before we arrive, will you tell me one more thing, Gracie?"

"If I can." Her face tightened, as if she was bracing for bad news.

"Are we still married?"

"Yes."

"You don't wear a ring." He glanced at his own hand, saw no band on his own ring finger. "Why?"

"Why what?"

"Why are we still married?" Dallas slouched against his seat, hating that he had to ask, but needing the information to build another piece of the puzzle. "You could have divorced me. They told me I was in the coma for over five years. That's a long time for someone to be gone."

Especially a husband.

"Believe me, I know exactly how long it's been." Bitterness tinged Gracie's voice in spite of her best efforts to pretend nonchalance.

"So why didn't you get a divorce?"

"Stop pushing me!" she snapped, then immediately shook her head. "I'm sorry, Dallas."

"It's okay." But it wasn't. He wanted to figure out why she hadn't let him go and found someone new.

"I don't have an answer for you. For a while I thought you'd come back, show up on the doorstep with some long-winded explanation about where you'd been, why you hadn't called."

"And when I didn't?"

"I didn't have the money to find out about how to get a divorce. I didn't have the money for anything." The dam holding back her anger broke. "I wasn't just sitting in a chair waiting for you to show up, you know. I had

to get on with my life. You were gone, my dad was gone.
I had to find a way to survive."

"I'm sorry." It didn't help, but at least now he knew.
"You wanted to, though, didn't you?'

He needed her to answer that.

"At one point, early on, I considered divorce." Gracie
steered toward a white house tucked under a weeping
willow. "It doesn't matter now, does it?"

"I don't know." Dallas pressed his hands flat
against his knees.

"This is my place." Gracie pulled up to the house,
taking great pains to align her vehicle perfectly with the
post in front before she shut off the motor. She climbed
out of the truck quickly, opened the rear door and lifted
out her parcels. She was halfway up the path, her
sandals rustling the pea gravel, before she noticed he
hadn't followed.

"Come on, Dallas. Let's go inside." Gracie waited
until he'd joined her. "This is what I call home now.
Elizabeth gave—"

The front door flew open. A miniature blond whirl-
wind appeared on the step, hopping up and down on one
foot. "Did you get it? Did you get it?"

Dallas glanced at Gracie. Love washed over her face.

"Yes, I got it. And I want you to meet someone. But
let's go inside first." She smiled at the little girl before
motioning for him to follow her. "I'll introduce you to
Elizabeth Wisdom."

"Hi, Gracie. We had a lovely afternoon together." A
tall, gray-haired woman stood by the kitchen counter.
She nodded at him. "I see you brought some company
along. Welcome to the Bar None."

"Thanks." This was the benefactor? To Dallas she looked more like a grandmother.

"Shall I leave you now, Gracie? Or do you need me a bit longer?"

"If it wouldn't be too much more of an imposition, I'd like you to stay, Elizabeth. This concerns you, indirectly." Gracie grabbed Dallas's arm and drew him into the living room.

He glanced around. There was not an item out of place. That deliberate neatness struck him as odd, especially with a child present. But then maybe the little girl didn't live here.

Elizabeth arched one brow before nodding. She studied Dallas as she took a seat on the white love seat. Foreboding rushed over him, but he pushed it away. The doctor had told him to be prepared for surprises. All he could do was silently pray for courage as he waited for Gracie to make the next move.

"Have a seat," his wife told him.

Dallas chose the big armchair. Perched on the edge, he felt as if his life teetered on the edge of a precipice.

"Who else is here, Mommy?"

Mommy? He blinked as his wife grasped one tiny hand and led the child to stand in front of him.

"Honey, I want you to meet Dallas." Gracie's pretty face went white. The next words threatened to choke her, but she forced them out anyway. "Dallas, this is Misty. My daughter."

"Dallas?" Misty's halting voice held uncertainty. Her fingers curled into Gracie's, seeking reassurance.

"Yes, sweetheart." Gracie's tear-filled blue eyes begged him to understand.

"Oh. Dallas was my daddy's name. Are you my daddy?" The tiny girl wearing a mussed blue dress touched his knee, and in doing so, grabbed hold of Dallas's heart.

His daughter. Misty.

Her voice was an immature imitation of her mom's. Feathery golden curls spilled to her shoulders. Also like her mother's. Perfect features in a sun-kissed face. Pink bow lips that didn't smile or frown.

But Misty was not all Gracie. The jut of her chin, the dimple that flickered to life at the edge of her mouth— he knew those were his gifts to her. He'd studied his own features in the mirror so often, trying to figure out who he was.

He was a father.

Dallas's insides melted in wonder and intense love as he gazed into eyes that perfectly blended Misty's parental heritage, not quite green, not quite blue.

"Mommy?" Misty murmured, her voice uncertain, hesitant.

"Yes, honey. Dallas is your daddy." Gracie's voice seemed to come from far away.

Dallas studied his daughter, wondered how Misty could know his name.

"I talked about you," Gracie murmured.

"My mommy told me a lot about you. Only she thought you were in Heaven." Misty stared past him, unblinking. "But you're not in Heaven. You're right here."

"Yes, I am." In that second Dallas understood what Gracie hadn't been able to say.

Misty was blind.

His heart cracked, but he refused to allow pain to

edge its way into his voice. Not now. Not while she waited for his reaction.

"It's very nice to meet you, Misty." Dallas touched her hand, allowed her delicate fingers to wrap around his own. "You're a very pretty girl. You look like your mommy."

"My mommy's beautiful." Misty's smile reappeared. "I want to be just like her."

"I'm sure you do." Uncertain if she'd accept a hug, Dallas kept his arms by his sides, leaving the decision to Misty. She stepped back, reaching toward her mother.

Gracie grasped her hand but did not try to draw Misty away from him. Dallas was grateful for that. He wanted to know more about his daughter, he just wasn't sure where to start.

"Are you sure you're my daddy?"

He nodded, realized Misty wouldn't see that. It would take time to get used to the situation, but even though he'd only met her, he knew he'd go to any lengths to protect this beautiful child.

My daughter.

"Yes, Misty. I really am your father. I'm Dallas Henderson." He glanced at Gracie, trying to silently communicate his appreciation for the way she was allowing them to find their own way.

"Oh." Misty frowned, bow lips pursed in a peevish frown. "Didn't you want to have a girl like me? Is that why you didn't come visit us sooner?"

Like me. The cautious question sent a message. Misty was afraid he wouldn't love her. Because she was blind.

The knowledge hit low and deep. Dallas steeled himself, turned his pain into a prayer, as he had ever since he'd woken from his coma.

*Oh, Lord, if only I'd been here for her, been able
to reassure her that I'll love her no matter what. Help
me now.*

"No, Misty. That's not why I didn't come." He knelt
in front of her, pushed a golden strand off her face. "I
couldn't come because I didn't remember anything
about your mommy and I didn't know how to find her.
That's why I never met you until now. I'm sorry."

Five years of his daughter's life had passed without
him, and there was nothing Dallas could do about that.
He had to focus on now, on what they could have—if
he handled this right.

"Are you all better now?" She bumped against his
arm like an awkward colt.

"Mostly all better. I would have come sooner if I
could have, Misty. Don't ever think I wasn't with you
because I didn't want to be."

"Okay." She stood silent for several moments. Waiting.

Though Dallas searched her face, he could not
discern her reaction to his words. She hid her emotions
well, just like her mother.

We need time together, Lord.

A whisper-soft sound from the love seat drew
Misty's attention. Dallas realized suddenly that though
she couldn't see, his daughter's heightened senses made
her aware of everything in the room. Misty would miss
very little.

"I have trouble with my memory," he explained. "It's
kind of…broken."

"Like my dollhouse," she said knowingly. "Your
voice is sad. You're not smiling."

"In my heart I'm wearing a very big smile," he told

her softly. "A little while ago I didn't know I had a daughter. Now I can hardly believe I didn't know it a long time ago." Dallas glanced at Gracie, saw the tears in her eyes and knew she had thought about this moment many times.

Probably feared it, too.

Which would explain her reluctance to bring him here without preparing her daughter ahead of time. For it was very clear to him that Gracie loved this child more than anything.

"Can I see you?" Misty asked quietly.

Gracie opened her mouth to explain, but Dallas shook his head at her. He knew exactly what Misty meant.

"Of course you can." When she held out her tiny hand, he took it and guided it to his face. "Go ahead, Misty."

The moment her baby-soft skin touched his cheek, Dallas closed his eyes and soaked in the sensations. Like stick men, her fingers walked over his forehead, slid around to "see" the shape of his face, the length of his nose, his cheekbones and his mouth. He smiled when she brushed his ear, and her fingers quickly slid back across his lips, found the dimple that matched her own.

"Mommy doesn't have these," she said.

Dallas blinked, studied his wife.

True, but Gracie had everything else a woman could ask for. A perfect figure, sun-streaked golden-brown hair that tipped up at her chin in a perky style. A model's oval face boasting a natural, barely tanned glow.

"You got hurt."

Misty's careful probing gentled on his scalp. She'd missed nothing.

"I hurt my head a while ago."

"Is it sore?" she asked, gently touching the rumpled edges of healed tissue buried just beneath his hairline.

"No, not anymore."

"How did you get it?"

"I don't know," he told her simply. "I can't remember."

Dallas glanced up at a wall of photographs. A picture of Gracie holding her brand-new baby forced home exactly what he'd forgotten. Until now he'd known he was missing details, but faced with the visual progression of his daughter's life, he suddenly realized the totality of what he'd lost and could never recapture.

Why, God?

"You're looking at my wall, aren't you?" Misty's chest puffed out.

"Your wall?" Stupid question. Dallas could clearly see that the pictures all centered on Misty. "Yes, I am. I never knew anybody who had a whole wall of their own. It's very interesting."

"*Interesting* is a word adults use when they can't think of anything else to say." Her fingertips brushed his cheek again before she dropped her arm to her side. "Mommy, did you get the part for my dollhouse?"

"Yes, I did. I put it on the counter by the cookie jar. Perhaps Elizabeth will help you. I want to talk to Dallas for a few minutes."

"Okay." Misty walked purposefully toward the kitchen, felt unerringly for the bag next to a brown ceramic bear, then shifted toward the love seat. "Elizabeth, will you please help me?"

So easily she dismissed him. Dallas wanted to weep.

"I'd love to help, dear. Though you'll have to show me what to do. I've never fixed a dollhouse before."

"Don't worry, I have. I know exactly how to do it." Misty paused in the doorway. "Will I see you later, Dallas? Is he staying for dinner, Mommy?"

"I'm not sure yet. We'll have to see. Be careful of the sharp places, honey."

"I'm always careful. You don't have to tell me so much," Misty grumbled before waggling a hand in his direction. "Bye, Dallas." She walked out of the room and down the hall.

Dallas. Not Daddy.

But then, he hadn't been her father. He was just a strange man who'd suddenly appeared in her life. Dallas didn't know who he had been, but in that moment he prayed he could be a good father to this special child.

"It's a bit late, but I'd like you to meet Elizabeth Wisdom, Dallas. She's been a wonderful friend to Misty and me."

"A pleasure to meet you." He shook her hand, patiently bearing her intense scrutiny.

"I'm glad Gracie found you." Elizabeth opened her mouth to continue, but Misty called to her. "I'm sure we'll talk later," the woman added.

Dallas wasn't sure if that was a promise or a threat, but he found an odd comfort in knowing that she cared enough for his family to check him out.

"I look forward to it." He watched her walk away, then turned toward Gracie. His wife.

How odd that sounded.

And how wonderful.

"Do you mind if we sit outside?" Gracie walked toward the kitchen. "I have some iced tea."

"Sure." Dallas followed, accepted a glass from her

and trailed behind through a set of French doors to a deck that overlooked a small green yard. To the left lay an oval pool. He whistled under his breath. "Nice."

"Yes, it is. Elizabeth has been very generous." Gracie pointed to a lawn chair. "Have a seat. I thought we could talk more freely out here."

"More freely?" he repeated.

"Misty's hearing is very acute. She's also very curious. I'd prefer we speak without her listening. For now."

Misty was a gorgeous child, bright, inquisitive. He wanted the chance to be more than a visiting stranger.

"Did your father know Misty?" he asked.

Gracie's fingers clenched around the arms of her chair. She licked her lips, but it took another moment before she finally spoke. "She was born two weeks after he died."

So she'd had a newborn to care for all by herself.

"I wish I'd been there, Gracie. I wish I could have helped you."

After a moment her color returned. She sipped her tea. "It wasn't your fault."

"Maybe not. But still." Dallas wasn't sure how much to ask, but curiosity forced the question from him. "Was Misty blind from birth?"

Gracie nodded. "Nobody knows why. The pregnancy was normal. There were no indications, no reason for it."

But she'd had a hard time. He could see it written all over her face.

"When did you find out?"

"The day after she was born. I had a Caesarian. I don't remember much about the first night. The next morning they did a battery of tests. I hoped and prayed someone had made a mistake, that they'd find a cure, that there was an operation that could change it." A wry smile twisted her lovely lips. "There wasn't. Misty is blind and nothing can change that. Or the fact that I love her."

"That's obvious. So is the fact you've found a way to help her enjoy her life, to experience everything she can."

"Not everything. Some things she will never do. I've accepted that. Now I try to keep her environment as safe as possible, to protect her."

A sense of dread underlay Gracie's words. Dallas wanted to know why.

"Which means? Surely on a ranch that's especially for blind children Misty isn't in any danger?"

"It's not just for blind children. There are a number of disabled kids the Bar None works with." Gracie avoided his stare. "But that's why I accepted Elizabeth's offer to work here for six months. It's an opportunity to prepare Misty for the future. I want to make sure she gets every opportunity to handle the challenges she'll face."

"I imagine that's normal for every mother." The niceties were finished. He set down his glass and leaned forward. "You really wanted to come out here so you could ask me questions, Gracie. Go ahead."

"I have thousands," she admitted.

"Start wherever you like."

"Why don't you tell me what happened when you woke up in hospital?"

Dallas never thought about that day if he could help it. But Gracie had asked a question. At the very least he owed her whatever explanation he could offer.

"Apparently I suffered some kind of head trauma. My body had pretty much healed by the time I woke up. I knew how to read and write, I could answer normal questions." He grimaced. "It took a little longer to accept that I'd lost a huge amount of time."

"And that no one had come looking for you?" she prodded softly.

If only she knew how that hurt.

"At first I fussed about it. And a lot of other things. But one day, before I was released, I met a woman. She'd just lost her husband and she was going to the chapel. She knew about me—knew I'd been in the coma. Probably everyone in the hospital did." He'd hated being medicine's newest case study. "Anyway, she invited me to pray with her."

An expression Dallas couldn't interpret flitted across Gracie's pretty face. Then she pulled her mask back into place.

"Go on."

"I went with her. There wasn't a lot to do in the hospital. I was well, except for my memory. I was sick of the never-ending tests and I was bored."

"I guess that's as good a reason as any to go to church."

Dallas laughed at her comment.

"It's not a very good reason at all, Gracie. But that's why I went. Only it wasn't a church. It was a chapel. A quiet sanctuary amidst all the suffering."

Lilies. He remembered Easter lilies. As soon as he'd pushed the solid oak door open their aromatic blooms had gorged his senses.

"I sat with her and I felt this peace, solemnity, if you want. After a while I noticed a verse written in some kind of calligraphy across one of the lit windows. It was from Romans and the last part of it said, '…and we confidently and joyfully look forward to becoming all that God has had in mind for us to be.'"

"I see." Gracie studied him the way a nurse observes a psychiatric patient.

"I know it's hard to understand, but I sensed a kind of reassurance that no matter what, God would take care of me. I still knew Him and He knew me."

That moment would stay with him for the rest of his life, but Dallas couldn't expect someone who hadn't lived through those horrible, empty black spaces to understand.

"And?"

"And He did. The woman came back and asked the hospital to let me work with her at an animal shelter. There was a whole lot of discussion, but finally some government agency worked out temporary identification and a place for me to stay. I earned a little bit of money. When the dreams started getting clearer, I told them I had to go. I came to Dallas on the bus. The rest you know."

"So the dreams didn't come till after?"

Dallas shook his head, struggling to make her understand. "From the day I woke up I began to see things, hear things. When I fell asleep they got clearer. Some I've managed to figure out. Some drive me crazy." He paused, then admitted, "The worst is Mini Belle. As far as I can tell, it's either a cheese or a car."

Gracie doubled over in laughter.

Dallas stared at the transformation. His wife was gorgeous. Her whole face glowed. He could not look away.

But when the laughter continued too long, he frowned. "Mind sharing the joke?"

"Mini Belle isn't a car or a ch-cheese," Gracie sputtered.

"What is it then?" He felt stupid, awkward, out of place. He hated not getting the joke, or wondering if he was the butt of it.

"Mini Belle is a horse." Grace sniffed, dabbed at her eyes. Seeing his disbelief, she nodded. "A miniature horse that was particularly fond of you. You once told me she greeted you by pressing her left front hoof on the toe of your boot until you gave her a carrot."

He listened as she explained about his work with the miniature horse association in Arizona, how he'd studied the friendliness of the small horses.

"What other words have been bothering you? Maybe I can help?"

He decided to risk it.

"Fala-bella? I'm not sure I have the pronunciation quite…" Dallas stopped. He could tell from her face that she recognized the word.

"Falabella. It's a very rare breed of miniature horse. Originally they were found only on the Falabella Farms in Argentina. I think now there are about nine hundred worldwide. In fact, we have one here at the ranch," Gracie told him. "It was a gift from a South American group for Elizabeth's help with some Amazonian issue."

"Oh." So it was work he'd been thinking about all these months. Hope deflated. He'd prayed for some clue that would unravel the past, something to link him with Gracie and Misty. This was not it.

"What else?" she asked quietly.

"Porter. I keep hearing the word *porter.*"

"Ray Porter was your boss. He's retired now."

Dallas wanted something more personal, something that would define who and what he'd been, what he'd done with his life, what meant the most to him. He told her more, but every time he repeated a word or described a dream, Gracie related it to work. Finally he chose the one that bothered him most. "Regret."

"You mean you have regrets?"

He shook his head. "No, it's like a title I see on the wall of my mind. Regret."

"Could be anything." Gracie shrugged. "You probably regretted having to leave home that last day. We'd only been married a week, but you had a meeting in Washington State, and then somewhere near Santa Fe, I think. You said you couldn't miss them. Maybe regret was the last thing you felt."

"When I see 'regret' I don't feel emotion," he explained, searching to understand why that word seemed so important. "It's more like a tangible thing."

"I don't know how to help you." Gracie frowned. "I suppose we could phone Ray and ask him if the word has any significance. But I'm not sure he would know more than that. You had almost finished your contract with them. You worked freelance."

Dallas felt certain that wasn't the answer he was looking for. But Elizabeth appeared at that moment.

"You must stay at the ranch as long as you like, Dallas." The woman's warm smile chased away the anxiety clawing his insides. "I don't know what your accommodation arrangements are, but you're welcome to stay in what I call the bunkhouse with some of our other employees. And if you need a job, we could certainly use you. How are you with horses?"

"He's an expert," Gracie said, before Dallas could admit he didn't know.

Between the two ladies they had his future nailed down in two minutes. It was like being trapped between whirlwinds, but Dallas didn't mind. He felt relief that he could stay, get to know his wife and daughter. Somehow God would reveal the next step.

"I'll ask our sheriff to come over a little later. He's a friend of mine and I'm sure he'll help us figure out a way to locate your family." Elizabeth surveyed his shabby clothes. "Camp staff usually wear jeans and camp shirts, which we provide. You can pick some up tomorrow morning, or Gracie can show you this evening. She'll know where to find some boots, as well."

Though he searched her face, Dallas found no hesitancy in Elizabeth's manner toward him. The ranch owner obviously valued Gracie's opinion and would accept Dallas on her word.

"I'll do my best to make sure you're not disappointed," he promised. But Elizabeth didn't return his smile.

Her brown eyes darkened.

"Don't worry about disappointing me," she murmured, an iron inflection backing the softly voiced words. "Worry about them." She inclined her head toward the house, where Gracie had run inside to answer Misty's call. "They're more important than anything."

"I know that. It will be hard for Gracie to have me back after such a long time," he admitted.

"But you will stay?"

"Ms. Wisdom, you couldn't pay me to move, now that I've found my family."

"Good. God created families to support and love each other. He's brought you here for a reason, Dallas. I'm going to pray you find it."

"Thank you."

Elizabeth patted his shoulder, then walked out of the yard toward the main buildings, whistling a little tune as she went.

Dallas sank back into his chair and sipped his tea, watery now that the ice had melted.

"I sure hope You know what You're doing here, Lord," he said, trying to ignore the call Gracie's swimming pool sent his weary body. "Because I haven't got a clue."

He tilted his head back, closed his eyes and waited for the shadows to come. But for the first time since he could remember, no whispers haunted him.

Chapter Three

Gracie swam through the pool with smooth, easy strokes, stretching every muscle, hoping the effort would clear her mind, leave her body limp and ready to rest.

So far it was not working.

Earlier, Elizabeth had insisted her personal physician come out to the ranch, examine Dallas and contact the hospital that had cared for him in Los Angeles. Only after the doctor had certified that Dallas was physically fine had Elizabeth allowed the meeting with her sheriff friend. He'd already been in contact with the L.A. authorities who'd questioned Dallas extensively when he'd first awakened. But L.A. had little to pass on other than that he'd been found unconscious, without identification, and no one had called to inquire. The sheriff left after offering to help locate Dallas's parents.

Gracie had decided it would be easier, and less taxing on her emotions, if they all ate dinner in the big mess hall with the rest of the staff and some of the regular students. That knocked Misty's routine off-kilter, so it took a while to answer her many questions and get her into bed. By then Dallas had gone with Elizabeth to inspect his new quarters, and Gracie was alone in her house.

All she could think about were Dallas's parents and how long it would take the sheriff to find them.

How long she had until her world changed again.

Now, here in the dark, with only a few yard lights glowing in the distance, and a big Texas moon overhead, Gracie could finally admit what a shock she felt.

Dallas was back.

Her entire body recognized him with a burst of longing. Her skin knew his voice. Even her eyes couldn't tear themselves away from watching him. But in her heart Gracie knew this wasn't the man she'd loved. This wasn't the husband who knew her thoughts before she said them, who'd shared her dreams.

Gracie had spent the past six years burying memories. She'd worked long and hard to finish her training. She was on the cusp of achieving the future she'd struggled so hard to reach.

Why was Dallas back now, when she'd finally found a safe place for Misty to grow and experience life? And worse, how long would he stay?

Not that Gracie wanted Dallas to leave. She couldn't stop imagining his arms around her. She yearned to hear his low whispers of love once more, ached to finally have the family she'd dreamed of.

It would have been easier if she could hate Dallas, if he'd done something hurtful, deliberately abandoned her, disowned Misty. But he hadn't. He'd simply lost his memory.

This afternoon Dallas had gone to great lengths to reassure Misty.

But he wanted more.

Gracie knew it as surely as she knew that six years ago she'd given him her heart.

That was then.

She couldn't afford to love again.

Nights were the worst.

That's when shadows crept out from their hideaways and ghosts from an unseen past teased.

Walking was Dallas's preferred therapy. In L.A. he'd walked through the hottest days, through rainstorms, through the smoke from hill fires. He walked as long as his body would keep going, until he could finally collapse in sleep.

At every bus stop on the way here he'd gotten out and walked. He'd walked as hard and as fast as he could to stop the thoughts from swarming his brain. He'd walked until his body weakened and he had to hide in a corner of the bus stop coffee shop and sip tea while his limbs recouped.

Anything but dream.

Tonight was no different, except that here on the ranch, Dallas felt freer to wander. Elizabeth had said he could go almost anywhere he pleased. There would be a lot of speculation tomorrow. Curious staff would have questions. But he'd gone through that in the hospital. People soon gave up asking questions when you had no answers to give them.

Tonight he walked briskly, savoring the soft night breeze and the scents it carried. The ranch boasted a glass-walled indoor facility with hydro therapies, whirlpools, training pools—he couldn't remember what else Misty had told him about. He passed that building, came to an outdoor pool surrounded by a fence hidden by prickly rosebushes. Not only would the thorns prevent the seeing and physically impaired from stumbling into the pool, but the heady scent of the paths differed in texture, so that footsteps made distinct sounds on each. Yet all were built to accommodate wheelchairs, crutches, canes and scooters. Sweet-scented floral borders also worked as a signal—lavender to the left, alyssum to the right. Children like Misty would soon learn independence.

Dallas chose a path that bordered the playground. He meandered through it, not bothering to examine the state-of-the-art equipment as he allowed his thoughts to roam where they wanted.

They wanted to think about Gracie.

Beautiful Gracie, who couldn't or wouldn't let herself relax. Surely all her fear wasn't due solely to Misty's situation. If only he could remember something about their past, something that would help her.

After relentlessly probing his locked brain for answers it wouldn't release, Dallas glanced up and realized he'd walked in a circle toward Gracie's house, this time approaching from the rear. He saw glints of pool reflections on the house, heard a lone swimmer cut through the water in a steady rhythm.

So Gracie couldn't sleep, either.

Dallas didn't call out, chose instead to muffle his steps on the grass beside the path. She always managed to mask her expression when she looked at him. He needed to catch her unaware, to discern what was really going on behind that beautiful facade, to see whether she hated him for coming back.

Gracie swam with the same lithe grace she did most things. Only her head was visible, her hair a slick silver helmet in the moonlight. The pool lights had been dimmed, the yard light switched off.

Dallas watched wordlessly until she finally climbed from the pool, toweled herself off.

"You don't have to stand in the shadows, Dallas. There's a latch on the gate at this end. You can come in if you want."

Now he knew where Misty got her acute hearing.

"Sorry." He let himself into her yard, shame burning his cheeks. "You must think I'm a Peeping Tom."

"I think you probably have a thousand questions and couldn't sleep because of them."

"Is that your excuse?"

"I like to swim at night." She pulled on a thick terry robe, motioned him to a chair. "I made some mint tea. Would you like a cup?"

"No, thanks." He watched her pour steaming liquid from a thermos. "Do you swim at night a lot?"

"If I can." She cupped the mug between her hands, studied him from behind the steam that rose from it. "I've always loved the water, and this is the first time I've had a pool in my own backyard. My days are filled, and when Misty comes home I'm busy with her. Nights seem the best."

"Surely you have some free time?" He couldn't accept that she'd been locked away from life for the past six years, not a beautiful woman like her.

"Misty is a full-time job."

One he'd missed.

"Misty is five now, right?"

"Her birthday was in February."

"Surely that's old enough to allow you some freedom. From what I saw today, the children who use this facility are taught to become independent."

"There is always someone watching them. Maybe you missed that." An edge crept into Gracie's voice, a defensiveness he hadn't counted on. Or maybe he was the problem.

"Did I do something wrong, Gracie?"

"Why do you ask that?"

"Because it feels like I'm walking through a minefield."

"It's not you, Dallas." Defeat weighted her shoulders, added to the dullness of her eyes. "It's just…" She shook her head, sipped her tea. "It doesn't matter."

"Yes, it does. I'm her father. Your husband." How strange that sounded. "I want to know if I said or did something that was out of place or hurt her. Or you."

"It's not you, Dallas. It's Misty. She's blind."

"Yes." He nodded. "I know."

"But do you realize what that entails?" Gracie set down her cup. "I'm her security. I'm who she turns to when something's wrong in her world. I can't decide one afternoon that I need a time-out, and disappear."

"You did this afternoon."

She shook her head. "That was different. And besides, Elizabeth was here. Misty is always cared for when I work. I never leave her alone."

"I'm sure you're a great parent. But I'm here now. I can help."

"You're the problem."

Her comment hit him squarely in the chest. She didn't want him here.

"Fine. I'll leave tomorrow morning, if that's what you want." Dallas clenched his jaw, swallowed his anger. "But I will continue to see my daughter. Now that I've found Misty, I'm not walking away from her."

"I don't want you to go!" Gracie shook her head. "That's not what I mean."

"Then you'd better explain," he snapped, frustrated by the dead ends he kept running into. "Because I am completely lost. As usual."

Her quick gasp, the way she huddled into her chair, her drawn miserable face struck him deeply, and his heart relented.

Dallas knelt in front of her, wrapped his hands around hers and waited for her to look at him. When she did, tears glittered on her lashes. He released one hand, lifted his fingers and brushed the wetness away, fingertips tingling at the contact with her skin.

"Gracie, I'm not trying to push you out of the way or take over. You've spent five years raising our child and I haven't been here much more than five hours. I wouldn't dream of undermining you. Why would I? You've done a wonderful job. She's a daughter any man would love to call his own."

A tremulous smile curved Gracie's mouth briefly. "Thank you."

He touched the damp strands that tumbled forward, pushed them away from her eyes so he could see more clearly. "I only want to share Misty with you."

"I know." She cupped her palm against his jaw. "I

understand you want to help. But that brings its own problems."

"Why?" Using every ounce of strength he had, Dallas resisted the urge to lay his head on her knees.

"Because Misty will want more." Her hand pulled away from his, the other dropped from his cheek.

A keen sense of loss washed over him.

"From the time she could speak, Misty has talked about wanting a family. I try to give her everything, but I can't give her that." Gracie stopped, chewed her bottom lip. When she spoke again her voice had dropped. "I also can't guarantee that you won't hurt her."

"I won't."

"Not intentionally, maybe, but when your memory comes back..." She met his gaze and did not look away. "I don't want my daughter to suffer, Dallas."

"I'm not going to hurt her," he declared angrily, then told himself to calm down. She was a mother protecting her baby. "But nobody gets through life without some scars, Gracie."

"I know that. Yet it's hard to explain to a five-year-old." A winsome smile tilted her lips up at the corners. "Awfully hard."

"I'm sure. But your point is moot. I'm not going anywhere. And we already are a family."

She shook her head slowly. "We were never a family," she murmured, a note of sadness lacing her voice. "We didn't have time."

The words were devastating to hear.

Dallas had longed for things to be the way they had been before—when he assumed his life had been normal, had made sense. But did he even have what it would take to be a father to Misty, to one day be the kind of husband Gracie wanted, needed?

The past months had taught him many things, foremost that he was not a quitter.

He rose, stood in front of his wife and stated his case. "Until someone or something forces me to go, I will be here, Gracie. For you, for our daughter. I'm not leaving."

"But—"

"I want to know everything about Misty. I want to watch her grow, change, learn, live. I want to be her daddy. I won't run away and I won't walk out. But whether we'll be a family is up to you."

She stared at him, silent, brooding.

"I know I'll fail sometimes. I'll make mistakes, do the wrong thing, and probably make you angry, too. But I won't work against you and I won't pit Misty against you. I don't remember who I was or know what you expect of me. But I do know I am going to learn how to be a part of her life. Because I will not give up my daughter. Not ever."

Dallas turned and walked away, into the darkness, where he could deal with the shadows in his life without anyone watching.

Alone in the gloom, Gracie contemplated her future long after Dallas had left.

One chance encounter in the city and their entire world was changed.

The future Gracie had so carefully planned, the protection she showered on her daughter, the devotion she hoped would make up for any shortcomings—what would any of that matter now that Dallas was in the picture?

Gracie loved Misty, but she also understood human nature. Her little girl would soon want more than the basics her mom could offer. Once Dallas discovered his parents' wealth, he'd shower Misty with everything Gracie could never afford to match. Her daughter's days of contentment wouldn't last much longer.

Neither would her own.

It was kind of Dallas to stay however long Misty needed him, but Gracie couldn't let herself believe him. Not again.

She didn't dare.

Dallas had loved his work, loved the excitement of traveling to each new place, seeing new faces. That first week they'd been married, he'd stuck around her father's home in North Dakota for three whole days before he'd found a llama in the next county that demanded investigation.

Recalling that, Gracie's insecurities resurfaced. She had reasons for feeling skeptical—Dallas's past refusal to pin down their future.

"You're working with your dad. He needs you. I understand that, sweetheart. And I need my work. But I also need you." He kissed her nose. "Don't worry about tomorrow or next week. We've got now. I'll have to go away from time to time, at least until this contract is over. But I'll always come back."

The very next day he'd disappeared for six years.

And she'd been left to listen to lectures from her father about the foolishness of love, repeated weekly until the day he died.

"I don't know what idiocy caused you to marry someone who can't even give you a home. Someone who's on the run all the time."

"He's not on the run, Dad. And this is his home. I didn't want to leave you in the lurch. It was Dallas's idea that I stay with you while he's on the road. In the fall I'll be back at college. We'll work out something different then."

"If he lasts that long."

She could never forget the slams against her new husband, the sneers when Dallas didn't come home, the outrage when she'd announced her pregnancy.

All the prayers Gracie could muster hadn't brought Dallas back.

Until now.

Why now?

She tossed her cold tea under an azalea bush. Memories belonged in the past. There were too many things to worry about in the present.

"How long is Dallas going to be here?" Misty fiddled with the toast squares Gracie had smeared with honey and peanut butter.

"I don't know, sweetie." She tiptoed through this new territory. "For a while, I think."

"'Cause we're his family, right?"

"Mm, sort of. He also has a mom and a dad, so he has extra family."

"You mean I have a granny and a grandpa?" Misty's cute smile lit up her whole face. "Yes!" She punched her fists toward the ceiling in celebration.

Then doubt bullied its way in.

"Why don't they come and see me?" she asked, her voice diffident, as if she was awaiting bad news.

Whoops. Gracie bit her lip, scrambled for a way to explain the inexplicable past.

"Don't they want me for their granddaughter?"

"Oh, sweetie, that's not why." Gracie hugged her cuddly daughter close and prayed she wasn't lying. "I don't think they even know about you. I haven't seen them since before you were born."

"Oh." Misty stayed still for a moment, then patted Gracie's cheek before reaching for another slice of toast. "Do you think Dallas likes me?"

"Dallas loves you, Misty."

Gracie whirled around, saw him lounging against the screen door. He lifted an eyebrow and she nodded, granting him permission to enter.

"How are my two beautiful ladies this lovely morning?"

"I'm not a lady." Misty giggled. "And I don't think I'm pretty. Rory Donovan said I was ugly, and dumb, too, 'cause I don't know how to ride a horse."

"Rory Donovan must need glasses. Trust me, you're very pretty, Misty."

"Rory doesn't need glasses!" Misty giggled again. "He can see good."

"Not that well, if you ask my opinion. And you can always learn to ride a horse, can't you?"

Gracie opened her mouth to nix that idea immediately, but Dallas was already seated next to Misty. He'd stolen a corner of her toast.

"You make a delicious breakfast, Misty."

"I didn't make it. Mommy did."

Gracie noted with surprise Misty's flushed cheeks. Her daughter was enamored of Dallas. But why should she be surprised? She'd been the same way herself.

"You don't make your own toast?" His own surprise was obvious in the look he directed at Gracie.

Gracie opened her mouth to explain, but Misty beat her to it. "I could do it if I tried," she blurted in self-defense. "But Mommy doesn't like me to touch hot things."

"I see."

Gracie felt the condemnation in his stare.

"Come on, sweetie. I've got to get to work and your class is going to start soon." She didn't have to explain her parenting style to him. Besides, Misty was only five. There was plenty of time for her to learn to do for herself.

"Can you get my backpack, Mommy?"

Gracie turned toward the bedroom, found her access blocked by Dallas.

"Don't you have to wash the honey off your fingers, Misty? You could get your backpack on the way, couldn't you?" Dallas winked at Gracie. "Your mom has to comb her hair. She's got a cowlick."

"Vets don't let cows lick their hair." Misty guffawed at his word choice. "Anyway, she hasn't even gone to work yet."

"A cowlick is when your hair stands up in places it's not supposed to. And your mom's got three of them. Or maybe I should have called it bed head. Anyway, she's got it. You'd better get your own backpack because it's going to take her a long time to get her hair fixed."

Misty carried her plate to the counter, set it down, then paused. "I thought you said you forgot stuff. How do you know how long it takes ladies to fix their hair?"

"Boys learn about that at a very young age," he said, visually daring Gracie to contradict him. "And trust me, they never ever forget. Not if they're smart. If you don't take all day washing your hands, I'll walk with you. Would you like that, Misty?"

"Sure." She hopped from one foot to the other. "Today's the first day of classes. No more babysitters."

Gracie smiled at her daughter. Misty insisted babysitters were for babies, and had loudly protested the hours she'd spent at day care, while the teaching staff arrived at the ranch.

"Okay. I'll walk you there. Then I've got to get to work."

"Okay." Misty skipped down the hall, humming a little tune as she went.

Gracie grabbed the opportunity.

"I'd appreciate it if you didn't start questioning our arrangements, Dallas." She walked to the mirror and smoothed her hair. "Our system works for us."

"It works for you, maybe," he argued. "It wouldn't hurt Misty to do things for herself. Isn't that the whole point of this place, to get the kids to learn independence?"

"Of course. But we've only been here a week, and she's not that familiar with everything here yet. So back off, Dallas," Gracie hissed as the child's footsteps clattered toward them. "Ready, honey?" She savored a last mouthful of coffee, ignoring him.

"Yes. Did you get your hair fixed?"

"It's as good as it's going to get," Gracie told her.

"Misty, I need to talk to your mom about something. Can you wait for us at the gate?"

Gracie caught her breath and stepped forward, but Dallas's hand on her arm and the quick shake of his head stopped her.

"Okay."

"Do you know how far it is?"

"Seven steps." Misty sounded offended. "Only Mommy doesn't allow…" Her voice trailed off.

"This time it's okay for you to go to the gate by yourself, honey." Gracie fumed at Dallas's impudence. Only last night he'd promised not to interfere. "But only go to the gate. Don't undo it."

"I know. I know." She walked to the door, grabbed the knob and yanked it open. "I'm not a baby, Mommy."

"Of course you're not."

Gracie waited till Misty was halfway down the walk before she turned on Dallas. "What exactly are you doing?"

"Trying to understand you." His lips quivered with the start of a smile. "Gracie, you can't be there for every single move she makes. You've got to teach her how to function independently. What would happen if she had an accident or an emergency? Misty needs to know exactly what she should do and how to manage on her own."

"We *manage* just fine, thank you." *Or we did, before you came on the scene.*

"I was told Misty's the only child her age whose mother walks her to the day care." He kept his voice low, but that didn't disguise his irritation. "How do you think that makes her feel?"

"I told you, we've only been here a week! Give us a chance. I haven't had time to ensure—"

Dallas shook his head, holding her gaze with his own. "It's not the length of time I'm referring to, and you know it. What I don't understand is why you don't want your daughter to be more autonomous. Why you keep her so dependent on you when she's smart and more than capable of learning to manage on her own."

"What I don't understand is how you think you have the right to swoop in and tell me how to handle my child."

"Mommy!"

Gracie peered out the window checking on Misty. She was okay, for now. Gracie didn't bother to disguise her anger, as she stated, "Listen to me, Dallas. This isn't one of your studies you can manipulate to figure out how to maximize results. I'm her mother and I'll decide how much freedom she gets and when she can push the boundaries. I'm perfectly capable of raising my child without your advice, just as I have for the past five years."

She'd gone too far and she knew it.

Dallas's face blanched. He reared back as if she'd slapped him. He never said a word, simply walked to the door, pulled it open and stepped outside.

"Are we going now, Dallas?"

"In a second, Misty. Soon as your mom's ready." No trace of irritation or anger slipped through the smooth, even tone.

"I'm glad you came, Dallas." Misty threaded her tiny fingers into his.

"So am I."

Gracie emerged from the house a few seconds later to find Dallas and Misty bent head to head, discussing how many posts there were along the sidewalk to the main building.

"You probably can't count that high," he challenged, ignoring Gracie.

"Can so." Misty smacked her hands on her little hips.

Despite her anger at him, Gracie almost laughed out loud. Dallas had just run up against the same stubborn streak that lay beneath his own easygoing exterior. She leaned against the door and watched.

"How many are there then?"

"Thirty one." Misty glared at him. "I counted yesterday with Mommy."

"Really?" Dallas ruffled her hair. "Good for you. I don't think I could count that high when I was five. You're way ahead of the game."

A gong echoed nearby.

Misty gasped. "My school is starting. I have to go. Emily will be waiting."

Gracie noted Dallas's raised brow. "Emily is her attendant," she told him quietly. "Each child has a specific person assigned. It makes them feel more secure. She met Emily yesterday morning."

"Got it." He nodded, but the warm glow she'd glimpsed earlier had been doused. "Let's go."

They walked together with Misty in the lead, widening the distance between them with every step she took. Gracie opened her mouth once to call her back, but Dallas caught her arm, shook his head.

"Doesn't she know the way?" he murmured.

"Of course she knows it!"

He raised one eyebrow. Since her daughter was already at the gate leading into the school, Gracie abandoned the argument, unwilling to admit it was she who felt ill-equipped to handle this next stage of development. For so long she and Misty had only each other.

"Hi, Emily," Misty crowed, showing her confidence that Emily would be there, as she had promised.

"Hello yourself. Did you sleep in?" The young woman glanced at Dallas curiously.

"I was up early. My daddy came to see me."

Gracie caught her breath at the ease with which Misty had accepted Dallas.

"I heard about that. You are a lucky girl." Emily nodded. "Dallas and I met last night." She waited for Misty to reach her side. "See you later," she said before they hurried inside.

Gracie watched her baby with regret and with joy. Misty was growing more confident, more comfortable. Leaving North Dakota and the friends who'd seen them both through some tough times had been difficult, but it had been the right choice.

"Are you going to the barn?" Dallas's quiet question broke through her thoughts.

"Yes. I've got a mare that's due to foal anytime."

"Isn't it late in the season?"

"Maybe, but I had no control over that." Gracie picked up her pace, heard him catch up. "Aren't you going to work?"

"Trying to get rid of me?" he challenged, a hint of mirth underlying his words.

As if she could.

"Elizabeth assigned me to shadow you, do whatever you told me to."

She frowned at him. "Why?"

"Maybe she thinks we need the time together. I

don't know. Do you want me to ask her for something else to do?"

Gracie thought about it for three seconds, quickly shook her head. There would be enough gossip about them circulating through the ranks. No need to add to it.

"Okay then." He followed her into the barn. "Tell me what to do."

The morning went better than Gracie had expected. Dallas anticipated her needs so well she managed to finish her work half an hour earlier than usual.

"Now what?"

"Elizabeth just bought a horse. She likes to rescue animals that have been mistreated, and this one definitely was. We need to check her out."

The mare whinnied at their approach, stomped hard to make her displeasure clear when Gracie undid the gate and stepped into her space.

"Stay back," she ordered. "Let me try to calm her. Two people will seem like a threat."

"Are you—"

"Just this once, do as I ask!" Gracie pulled the carrot from her pocket and headed toward the horse, too irritated to apologize for her outburst. "Hello, Lady. Feel like a carrot?"

Having already sniffed the treat in the air, Lady definitely was interested. Holding it out, Gracie coaxed her into an area of the corral where she had a better chance of getting close enough to check her wounds. But the mare had other ideas.

She allowed Gracie to touch her mane, but when the carrot wasn't forthcoming as quickly as she wanted, she pressed her head against Gracie's chest and knocked her onto her backside. Snorting with disdain, the horse pranced off, head high in the air.

"Are you all right?"

"Of course." Gracie accepted Dallas's hand up, ignored the knowing smirk tilting the corners of his mouth. "She's skittish, that's all."

"She's playing with you," he asserted.

"I suppose you have a better plan." He probably did, and that didn't bother Gracie. She only wanted to make sure the animal wasn't suffering.

"I don't know about a plan." Dallas's quiet tone surprised her. "I do have this idea…" His voice trailed away; his eyes clouded over. "Never mind. Maybe I should leave you alone. I'm sure you know what you're doing."

So did he.

Gracie sensed what caused his confusion. His natural skill with animals was coming back to him. Though Dallas might not recognize why he understood the mare's actions, she had seen her husband in action many times before, and knew Dallas simply understood animals.

"Go ahead. Try," she said encouragingly.

He hesitated. "I—I'm not sure what to do."

"Neither am I." Gracie couldn't ignore the plea for help he hadn't uttered. It hurt to see strong, confident Dallas so uncertain. She couldn't find it within her to let it last. "The worst she can do is knock you down. Go ahead."

He searched her face for a moment, finally nodded. "Okay, but if I mess up you'd better know how to do first aid."

"You won't need first aid. I have something that works better." She pulled a sugar lump from her pocket and handed it and the carrot to him. "I want to know if those sores on her sides are healing or if there's a sign of infection. If you can get her to stand facing me, as close as possible, I'll be able to get a good look."

He nodded, tucked the treats in his back pocket, then walked toward the suspicious horse, talking the entire time. Gracie couldn't hear all the words, but she recognized the soft conversational tone. Ears pricked up, Lady stood her ground, waiting while he moved closer. Eventually the mare caught the scent of the carrot, and though she snorted, she didn't shy away.

Dallas pulled the carrot from his pocket, broke off the end and held it out on his palm. Lady tossed her head, then reached out and snatched it from him. Dallas eased the remaining carrot back in his pocket and turned, began walking toward Gracie.

That wasn't what she wanted, and she opened her mouth to tell him so, until she caught a glimpse of his eyes and the message they were sending. *Trust me.*

It had been a long time since Gracie had really trusted anyone. But in that moment she couldn't forget the many times he'd said it to her during their weeks of long-distance courtship, each time he left, when he spoke about the future.

"Trust me, Gracie darlin'. We're going to have a future. It's just gonna take a while for us to get everything ironed out. But we will have a home of our own, a family. Trust me."

Gracie snapped out of her reverie at the sound of the horse's deep-throated gargle. She blinked, saw Lady butt Dallas in the back. The mare soon accepted his hand on her head, allowed him to touch her nose.

"Yeah, you're a little mixed up, aren't you? Just like me," he whispered.

Gracie focused on his face, on the tenderness blazing in his eyes.

"But we can get through it, girl." Dallas threaded his fingers through Lady's mane, but it was his voice that commanded the horse, not his hands. "We have to trust each other. You can let me in, can't you, Lady?"

Dallas led the horse nearer and turned her. "If you want to take a look, Gracie, this is as good a time as any."

"Keep talking and hold her as still as you can." Gracie moved slowly, checking the hooves as gently as she could. She went on to assess the long deep cuts a whip had made on the horse's ribs.

"Come on, girl. You're on show. You can do it." Dallas slipped her another morsel of carrot, and continued speaking. The mare calmed enough to allow him to scratch her ears.

"Okay, I've seen enough. I think she'll do. For now." Gracie walked back to the fence, let herself out and waited for him to follow.

But Dallas stayed with the horse, kept talking to her, handling her with light gentle touches that she tolerated a little easier each time.

Gracie couldn't look away from Dallas's face. He'd totally transformed from a pitiable amnesiac to a skilled rancher. No longer did he move hesitantly. Now he was in control, calm, his movements precise. He didn't jump back when Lady bumped his arm away from the sores under her neck, didn't fuss when she bared her teeth after he rubbed his hand down her forelock. He simply kept talking, winning her trust with soft words, gentle hands and an air of determination.

This was the real Dallas. It didn't matter whether he remembered or not. His skill, his gentleness… Gracie's eyes brimmed with tears as she remembered how he'd done the same with her, coaxed her into sharing her deepest desires, her biggest fears.

Dallas would work his magic on Misty, too. Gracie knew that as surely as she knew the sun would set. He was already more than halfway to winning the little girl's heart.

A gasp of awe drew her attention back to Dallas. A small crowd of children had gathered round to watch. He was now seated on Lady's back, bent forward over her neck so he could talk to her. She danced for a moment or two at the burden, then settled into a nervous trot. They went round and round in a circle until she was perfectly at ease. Only then did he slip from her back, pat her and offer the sugar lump.

By the time he left the paddock, the sighted kids were clapping. Misty clapped harder than all of them as Emily described the scene to her.

"That's my dad," Gracie heard her boast.

Dallas grinned at Gracie, bowed to the kids.

"Show-off," she chided, half in earnest.

"Sourpuss," he called back. When she didn't return his smile, Dallas faltered, frowned. "You didn't really mind, did you? I was just trying to help."

"I know." She turned, walked back to the barn.

Dallas was just trying to help with Misty, too. The question was, could he help himself to withstand his parents when they showed up here, demanding he take his place in the family business? And when they asked him to bring his daughter with him?

Gracie couldn't envision a worse scenario.

Chapter Four

"I can't talk about our past right now."

"Or last week, or last night. Why is that, Gracie?" Dallas shifted restlessly, frustrated by the roadblocks his wife kept putting up whenever he asked about their marriage.

"I have to prepare dinner for Misty. See you tomorrow."

Gracie hurried up the lane to her house, her back stiff with fear. If he let her, she'd push him so far away he'd never find his place in her life.

That was not going to happen.

Dallas was scared, too. He had no idea what he'd done in the past, how he'd treated her. But he'd promised God he'd do his utmost to build a relationship with his family. One week had only whetted his appetite to be with them more.

Dallas wanted, needed his wife back. But he had no memories to guide him. In the shadows of his mind a slew of questions grew. Maybe Gracie hadn't found him because she no longer wanted him in her life. Maybe that's why she wouldn't let him past the barriers she'd erected. Maybe, maybe, maybe. Every day was a balancing act as Dallas tried to rebuild his life.

He picked up his pace, followed his wife's model-slim jeans-clad figure through the front gate. "I could make dinner, Gracie." He grinned, feeling sheepish. "If you'll let me use your kitchen, that is."

"You?"

His impetuous offer had come with little forethought. Now Dallas wondered if he knew how to cook. Somehow that issue had not come up before.

No going back, he reminded himself.

"Yes, me," he agreed. "And Misty. I'll pick her up and we'll put our heads together while you take a break and relax. How does that sound?"

"Actually, wonderful. I never realized how demanding this job would be. The animals are terrific therapy for the children, but taking care of them is exhausting. Thanks for watching Misty last night while I stayed with that mare."

"My pleasure." If Gracie only knew how watching Misty's pink-flushed face as she slept reinforced his determination to regain his memory. "So the job's not what you were expecting?"

She tilted her head to one side, rubbed her neck. "I knew there'd be horses. The kids adore Clara the donkey and she's a sweetie. But the goat and the rest—it's a lot for one vet. Those tracks the wranglers saw on the crest of the hill yesterday aren't helping things, either."

"Why does that matter?"

Gracie turned to peer out the window at the hill. "I don't want any of the children endangered because a wild animal is tracking a sickly animal we have here."

She was worn-out with her worrying. Dallas saw it in her eyes and the tiny fan of lines around them, in the pinch of her lovely lips.

"Elizabeth has a lot of safeguards to stop that from happening."

An image fluttered through his mind. Of him standing behind her, massaging her shoulders, smoothing back her hair, whispering something that brought that gorgeous smile to her lips. As quickly as it appeared, the memory vanished, leaving him frustrated, aching to help but unsure how.

If only he could draw Gracie into his arms and smooth away the lines across her forehead. But he knew she wouldn't allow that. So Dallas offered the next best thing.

"Take a glass of iced tea and go out by the pool. Swim, sunbathe, whatever. All I ask is that you relax and don't come into this kitchen until I tell you. Let me take over for a while." He waited, knowing she couldn't let go that easily.

"It's kind of you, Dallas, but it's better if Misty and I stick to our routine." Gracie kept her head down, refused to look at him. "She finds it easier if things stay the same."

"Misty finds it easier?" he asked softly. "Or you do?"

"That's not fair." Her smoke-tinted eyes mirrored her hurt.

"I'm sorry. But I need time with Misty, Gracie." Dallas pressed his case. "I'm not trying to push you out of her life, but if you're always there, she'll never learn to trust me, and we won't be able to build a bond." He touched Gracie's cheek. "I promise I won't hurt her. I love her, too."

Her eyebrows lifted as if she doubted him.

"I loved her as soon as I met her," Dallas said, unembarrassed by the emotion coloring his voice. "Didn't you?"

"Yes." A wide smile transformed her tired face. "I did."

His beautiful, brave Gracie.

That's how he'd begun to think of her, he realized. As his. The part of him he was missing, a part he wanted back. He knew, in the deepest recesses of his heart, that he must have loved this woman. Every sense came alive whenever she was near. If only he could remember something.

The undeniable connection he felt toward Gracie strengthened with every encounter. When his hand brushed hers as they settled an animal, or when she accidentally bumped his shoulder while reaching for something. When they sat across the table in the dining hall during lunch or coffee and she inadvertently shared some tidbit about Misty's past. When Dallas lingered around the building, finding odd jobs so he could sneak glances at Gracie through the window while she worked on her records.

Despite all of that, she held back, keeping silent when he longed for her to pour out her heart about whatever troubled her.

Misty was the one door Gracie couldn't close, and Dallas had a feeling that if only he and Misty could really connect, his daughter would provide him with the way back to his wife.

He stepped forward now, smoothed back damp strands of her hair, cupped her cheeks in his palms. "You can trust me, Gracie."

She smiled, drew away, doubt clouding her eyes.

Dallas held his mounting frustration in check. He'd only known his daughter for two weeks. Gracie had been watching over her, protecting her, since her birth. Without him.

They both needed time to adjust.

"Please let me do this, Gracie."

She hesitated for so long he turned toward the door, defeated. Her soft whisper stopped him. "All right. But please be careful."

"Thank you." Joy erased restraint. Dallas turned back and brushed his lips across her cheek.

Though Gracie's head jerked as though she'd been singed by the contact, she didn't move away. Her hand covered the spot on her face and her voice betrayed the tiniest wobble as she said, "I know she's your daughter, Dallas. And I know you have every right to act as her father. It's just hard…" She stared at him. "I…can't lose her."

"Why would you lose her?" The pain in her voice twisted his insides, and he automatically reached for her, surprised when she allowed him to press her head against his shoulder. "There are two of us to watch her now, Gracie."

She felt right in his arms.

A familiar sweetness blossomed inside and he wondered how often he'd held her like this.

God, give me the words to say.

"Misty's strong and healthy. You've got a good job, a nice home, a great place for her to learn and grow. Isn't it time to stop being afraid?"

"I c-can't," she whispered.

He wanted to help her. Here was his chance.

"Misty's a beautiful little girl God gave to you. Why would you think He's going to take her away now?"

"I've always been afraid of losing Misty," she confessed, curling her fingers into his shirt.

"But why? God loves our daughter more than either of us ever could." Dallas rested his chin on her head. "You got through the tough times, Gracie. You did everything you had to. But you're not alone anymore. I'm here. I want to help you. If you'll let me."

She sniffed, drew back with her head bent. "You're a good father, Dallas. Misty loves having you in her world."

Gracie said nothing more, but the worry lingered in her eyes. What lay at the bottom of this fear?

"Tonight will be great. You'll see." He hugged her once, then set her free. "Misty will be wondering why I'm not there to pick her up," he added.

Gracie didn't look at him. But that was all right. Dallas understood she needed time and space to collect herself. He needed a few minutes, too, to figure out his own racing pulse, and the overwhelming urge to embrace her again.

"You go relax. We'll take our time coming back."

"But—"

He shook his head. "Trust me, Gracie."

"All right." Her eyes glowed richly blue. "But if you're not here in half an hour I'll coming looking for you."

"Yes, boss." Dallas saluted, walked toward the front door.

It's a start. Thank you, God.

But as he strode toward the building where his daughter would be finishing her last class of the day,

Dallas's feeling of satisfaction deflated when he turned and saw Gracie watching him.

Dallas's dark, rumpled head was the perfect counterpart to Misty's pale, wispy curls.

Gracie couldn't help but admire the way he helped her daughter build her confidence in the water. Nor could she help wishing she was back in the pool, with them, sharing the fun, instead of sitting on the side watching, like an outsider.

Oddly enough, it felt good to let someone else take over. Though Gracie refused to relax her watch.

Before Dallas's arrival, Gracie had seldom given a thought to her own needs. She'd focused completely on Misty, devoted herself to motherhood, done everything in her power to make sure her daughter had what she needed. It was all about Misty.

But now her maternal identity was being upstaged by a needy woman, one who wanted Dallas to notice she had taken special pains with her hair, and was wearing a pretty skirt and top to dinner. And a fresh floral perfume, so he wouldn't be reminded of smelly animals.

What Gracie wanted was for Dallas to spend just one moment really looking at her, the way he used to.

And yet she was afraid of that very thing, felt guilty for even thinking it.

Her first responsibility was to her child. Her daughter was the best thing that had ever happened to her, no matter what her dad had said.

"You can't even look after yourself. How can you care for a child?"

"I'll learn. Other women do it."

"Other women who have nothing else to do with their lives. I thought you were going to be somebody, to make something out of your life, not waste it on a fly-by-night man who only cared about you enough to sleep with you."

"Dallas isn't like that. Besides, we're married."

"So why isn't he here, supporting you?"

Gracie had never been able to answer that.

"She must be sleeping."

Droplets of water splashed on Gracie's face, drawing her back to the present so fast she jumped to her feet. "Hey!"

Misty's giggles echoed across the pool. "You weren't watching me, Mommy."

"I'm watching now." Gracie snatched up a towel. "Ready to come out?"

"No." Misty stood neck-deep in the water, her face alive with joy. "Me and Dallas want you to come in the pool with us. You said 'later.' This is later, isn't it?"

Dallas said nothing. Leaning against the edge of the pool, half-submerged, he watched her with those gorgeous hazel eyes that made Gracie's stomach do flip-flops.

Be careful what you wish for, she told herself.

Misty's pool toys surrounded her like a life preserver, proving that Dallas had paid attention to his daughter's twice weekly swimming lessons with Emily. He remembered that a blind child needed the security of those toys in the vastness of a pool. He was trying so hard to be what Misty needed.

"Come on, 'Mommy,'" Dallas said as he held up a hand to Gracie as Misty flopped down on a step and made swishing motions through the water with her hands, singing a little song about fish. "I promise I won't splash you."

"It's late," she began.

"It's Friday. Tomorrow is parents' visiting day. By the time the campfire and the meet-and-greet are over we won't have a chance to swim together. Come on."

He was pure temptation.

"All right. But just for a little while. It's almost Misty's bedtime." Gracie hurried away to change. When she returned, Dallas and Misty were head to head, discussing something. "What's up?"

"I want to swim all the way across the pool by myself."

"Misty, honey, I've told you. When you're a better swimmer—"

"I'm a very good swimmer now. Dallas said so." The stubborn chin lifted. "I want to try, Mommy. I'm not afraid."

No, but I am.

"What if we all go? Mommy will be on one side and I'll be on the other. That way if you need any help, you can just reach out and grab us."

"We'll be a team." Misty jumped off the step into the water and Dallas's waiting arms, ramming him with the floating toy she clutched. "Don't worry, Mommy. Dallas will help."

Which was exactly the problem. Gracie was afraid of his help, afraid of depending on it. Until now she and Misty had managed perfectly well. But with Dallas in the picture, everything changed.

It was no longer just the two of them. Dallas made Gracie question her decisions, just as he challenged Misty to push beyond the boundaries Gracie had set. Every day he eased into their lives a little further.

"You tell me the minute you feel tired, Misty," Gracie

ordered. "And when we get to the other side, that's it. Time for bed. No arguing. Agreed?"

"Oh, Mommy."

When no help came from Dallas, their daughter finally agreed to her terms. Once Gracie had removed the barricade that kept Misty in one corner of the pool, the little girl pushed off with a hearty splash that spattered both adults.

Misty did well until the halfway point, when she grew tired.

"You can't flop around like a walrus, kiddo. You're not wearing tusks," Dallas teased. He let her cling to his arm for a minute's rest, then encouraged her to set off again, resuming the swimming stroke she'd been taught.

He was a natural at fatherhood, Gracie decided as she paddled alongside, watching for signs of fatigue in the tiny body. No matter how many questions Misty asked him, he never seemed to run out of patience or encouragement.

"Way to go, Misty." Dallas hugged her close, then kicked back toward the steps, where he sat and let her rest on his knee. "You did it!"

"It was hard." She gasped for breath, her little chest rising and falling.

"Lots of things are hard. That doesn't mean we shouldn't try to do them."

"Why?"

Gracie's heart ached. Misty had overcome so many hard things already.

"If we don't try hard, we'll never know if we can or not. And then we'll be afraid."

"You are not to swim across the pool again unless I'm here and I say so, Misty. Understand?" Gracie caught the look Dallas shot her way, and floated toward the steps.

"Yes, Mommy," Misty said meekly. She clung to Dallas's neck, yawned. "Rory isn't going to believe I did it."

"Does that matter?" Dallas carried her out of the water, then held out a helping hand toward Gracie.

She accepted it, let him draw her up and out, ignoring her heart's little flutter.

"It matters." Misty was firm on that.

"Why?" Once Dallas had removed her personal flotation device and wrapped Misty in one of the big bath towels Gracie had supplied, he set her on a chair and toweled himself dry.

"Because Rory beats me at everything. Just once I want to beat him." Misty's voice grew softer. "I'm tired, Mommy."

"I know." Gracie pulled on her cover-up, slid her feet into her sandals. "Time for bed."

"Can Dallas carry me?"

"I—"

"Please? I don't want to walk."

"First we have to put your toys away," Dallas murmured.

"Mommy can do it," Misty said carelessly.

"No. Mommy's tired, too. She was working all day."

Gracie began unbuttoning her cover-up, to go back in the water to collect the toys, but Dallas rested a hand on her arm. "She has to learn to consider others, Gracie."

"She's tired. Besides, the deck is wet and slippery."

"She can walk on the grass." He turned to Misty,

grasped her hand. "Come on, Miss Misty, we'll make a chain gang. I'll send the toys to you and you carry them to Mommy. She'll be over by the fence. Do you know how many steps it is from the grass?"

"Fifteen." Misty rose from the chair, her curiosity roused. "But how are you going to send the toys to me?"

"Airmail. Hang on. I have to dive in to get that duck." Dallas did a mock cannonball that sent a wave of water splashing over both Misty and Gracie.

Face dripping, Misty doubled over in laughter. "Did you get it?"

"Go on the grass. Ready? Here's one duck flying to you, Misty." He tossed it through the air. It landed right at her feet. "Okay, pass it on."

Her fingers closed over the rubber. She walked across the grass, held out the duck. "Here, Mommy."

"Thank you, honey."

But Misty was already back in place, waiting for the next item.

Gracie held her breath as Dallas tossed each of the toys, but his aim was perfect. Not that the inflated things would have hurt Misty, it was just that Gracie was so used to making sure—

"Why don't you send more? I haven't had the beach ball yet."

Gracie met Dallas's stare, knew he'd seen her worry.

"Your mommy isn't ready. We have to wait for her to catch up."

"I'll help her." Misty moved across the grass easily, sidestepping Gracie. She felt for the toys and one by one dumped them into the bin. "I don't think you can make the ball fly over here, Dallas. It's too far."

She wore a teasing little grin that matched her father's so closely, Gracie got a pain in her heart.

"Is that a dare?" Dallas called.

"Yes."

"Okay, kid. You asked for it. Hold out your arms and stay still."

Misty obeyed, waiting expectantly for him to throw the ball. When it landed with a plop in her arms, water droplets splashed her face. She giggled as she tossed the ball in with the rest of the water toys. "You did it!"

"Of course I did." He scrambled out of the water, wrapped his damp towel around himself. "I'm very good at airmailing toys."

Gracie shivered at the memory of evenings they'd spent by the creek behind her father's house. Sweet lovely nights. Dallas mistook her shiver for cold and grabbed her towel, wrapped it around her shoulders.

"You'd better get changed. I'll look after Misty until you're ready." He snapped the pool gate shut behind him, then moved closer to Misty. "Let's get inside, kiddo. Soon as your mom's ready you can have a wash."

"But I'm not dirty."

Gracie hurried into the house, showered quickly and pulled on her jeans and a warm sweater. It had been hot today, but suddenly the air felt cooler.

She found father and daughter in the kitchen, still arguing about degrees of dirtiness.

"Come on, honey. Bath time." She allowed herself the merest glance at Dallas. "Misty will use my shower. You can have the other bathroom to change."

"But I want a bath, Mommy. I'm cold. Your bathroom doesn't have a tub."

Gracie squeezed her eyes closed. How to get out of this one? If Dallas went in her room he'd see the photographs she'd placed on the walls, photographs of him. He'd see the box he'd given her, and he was bound to notice all the mementos she'd stuffed inside. A dozen dried roses, a silver necklace, the only wedding picture she had.

Seeing her hesitation, Dallas shook his head. "It's fine, Gracie. I'll pull my jeans on and go back to the bunkhouse to change. But I'll be back in fifteen minutes to kiss you good-night, Misty. And you'd better be in bed."

Gracie hid her smile at her daughter's grimace.

"I'm leaving now, Misty," he added. "I bet I'm back before you're in bed."

"Come on, Mommy. I want to beat him." Misty tugged at Gracie's hand.

Dallas grinned at them, then hurried out the door. Suddenly the house felt empty, drained of the vitality Dallas always carried into a room.

"I will always love you, Gracie. No matter what happens."

If only love was enough.

Chapter Five

Dallas walked back to the house with more speed than was necessary.

But he couldn't seem to keep himself from hurrying, and it wasn't only because he wanted to kiss his daughter good-night.

Though Gracie was tired, he knew she would offer him something to drink. He intended to accept. And while he drank they could talk. Maybe he'd finally get some answers to the questions tormenting him.

He tapped on the door lightly. "It's me."

"I win!" Misty called from her room.

Gracie sent him a droll look from the kitchen, where she was pouring boiling water into a teapot. "Maybe you can get her to lie down, now that you're back," she said. "I doubt she'll go to sleep easily. She's overtired."

His fault.

"I'll get her to sleep." Dallas walked down the hall. "You relax. Read a book. We'll be fine."

Misty lay propped up in bed, waiting, her shining face uplifted. She giggled when he sat down beside her. "What does the winner get?"

"A good-night kiss?" He leaned over, placed a loud smack against her cheek. "How's that?"

"Mommy always reads a story to me." She pulled a dog-eared volume from the bookcase of braille books. "I like this one."

Misty couldn't know he'd been studying braille, though he wasn't proficient enough to read this yet. He heard a noise, saw Gracie standing in the doorway.

"I'll read it," she murmured.

"No, I want Dallas."

A flash of hurt lit Gracie's eyes before she shrugged. She opened her mouth to explain to Misty, but Dallas cut her off. "Actually, I thought I'd *tell* you a story. Is that okay?"

"I guess." Misty snuggled down in her bed to listen, the book still clutched in her fingers.

Dallas told the story of Daniel in the lion's den. It was the only one he could remember. By the time he'd finished, Misty was fast asleep. He studied her, his heart brimming with love, then bent and brushed a kiss to her cheek. As he rose the book tumbled onto the floor.

"Put it back," Gracie murmured. "So she won't trip on it in case she gets up in the night."

He did as she asked, then followed her from the room.

"Sorry, I forgot," Gracie said, pausing in the archway to the kitchen.

"Forgot what?"

"That you don't like mint tea."

"I think mint tea would be very nice right about now."

"Oh." She frowned, motioned for him to sit on the love seat.

Dallas settled there, reaching for the cup she handed him.

"How can you swim at night when she's sleeping? Aren't you afraid—"

Gracie held up what looked like a baby monitor.

"Oh." Here he was, sitting in her living room, and he couldn't think of anything to say. "Our daughter is an imp," he said, watching Gracie's face. Was it unfair to use Misty to get to his wife's heart?

"You hardly know she's blind sometimes. At her last assessment they said she was well ahead of her age group," Gracie told him.

"What I can't understand is why you're so afraid. Talk to me, Gracie."

She was silent so long he almost decided to leave. Then she rose and picked up the monitor, motioned to the patio doors.

"Little pitchers," she murmured.

Dallas followed her outside, sensing that it wasn't only Misty she was worried about. Gracie needed the cover of the night. He waited until she was seated on one of the lounges before pulling a second right next to it.

"What do you want to know, Dallas?"

Everything. Anything.

"When we were married, why did we go back to live with your father?"

"Because you said that would be best. The company gave you a place in Houston, but your work took you all across the country. You said I'd be alone too much, that it was better if I finished the spring and summer helping out my dad, that I'd have family nearby."

A shaky thread in her voice told him that hadn't been a good idea.

"Was your father happy about us?"

She looked at him, her eyes cold. "No."

"He didn't like me?"

"I suppose he might have liked you well enough, but he didn't like me getting married. I was supposed to finish my schooling. And when I found out I was pregnant…" She bit her lip.

Dallas sucked in a lungful of air. "Gracie, did he hurt you?" He gripped the side of his chair as he forced out the ugly words, anger spurting through him. "Were you abused?"

"Physically, no." She managed a quirky smile. "He wasn't like that. He would never have beaten me." She fiddled with the fabric of her top. "But he was very angry that we'd eloped, that I hadn't told him, and he made sure I knew it. Then when you didn't come back…" She stared at him, shrugged.

"Didn't I phone, e-mail?"

She nodded. "You called twice. Then I never heard from you again."

Dallas scowled at his stupidity. What man in his right mind would leave his bride and take off a few days after they'd been married? Especially a bride like Gracie. What was wrong with him?

"It's okay, Dallas," she murmured, her voice shaky. "I understood."

"Well, I don't. I think I was nuts." He had to relax,

let her tell her story her own way. "Go on. You found out you were going to have Misty."

"Yes. I could hardly wait to tell you. When you didn't come back, didn't call, I didn't know what to do. I phoned your boss, found out they'd been trying to locate you also. As far as anyone knew, the last place you'd been was Vancouver. You sent me a letter from there."

Vancouver? He couldn't visualize anything about the city.

"I was so scared something bad had happened. I didn't have any money to hire an investigator, and as the weeks went by with no news, it got harder to believe you were coming back. I started to believe what Dad said."

"Which was?"

"That I was too young to be a mother."

"We both know he was wrong about that." Dallas had to touch her, to make the contact that his body recalled even if his brain didn't. He brushed his hand over hers, entwined their fingers. "I think you're the best mother I've ever seen. Misty's a tribute to your work and determination."

"Thank you." She bowed her head. "I thought for sure you'd call at Christmas."

"Why Christmas?" He brushed his thumb over her silky skin.

"You told me it was your favorite time of the year, that you'd take me to Dallas and show me how Christmas should be celebrated. You had lots of plans. But you never came, and Dad and I spent Christmas as usual."

She sounded so sad. Another question popped up.

"What about my parents? Didn't I take you to meet them? We were married in Dallas, weren't we?"

Gracie nodded, but withdrew her hand and kept her eyes averted. "Yes, but they were away the day we got married. I had to get back home and you said we'd meet them another time." She paused, and when she spoke again there was an edge to her voice that Dallas didn't understand. "I contacted them before Misty was born, but they didn't know where you were, either, though they ran a big ad offering a reward for information."

There were pieces missing, things she wasn't saying, but Dallas let them go, anxious to get the broader picture settled in his mind.

"So you had Misty."

"After my father died. He had a heart attack." She bit her lip. "We'd been arguing. He always thought I'd take over his practice, and to do that I would have had to leave my baby with someone, go back to school and finish my training. I was scared and miserable and alone, and worried about raising a child without help, I couldn't promise him I'd do it, and he was furious."

Again the anger bubbled inside. What kind of a man put his pregnant daughter in such a position?

"You didn't cause his death, Gracie."

"It sure felt like it." She sniffed, rubbed her eyes and pretended to smile. "Anyway, he had a heart attack and died that night in the hospital. His funeral was held two days later. Two weeks later I went into labor, but it didn't progress so I had a C-section."

"I'm so sorry I wasn't there to help, Gracie." Dallas squeezed her hand, trying to express his feelings. "I'm sorry I went away without you, but I'm not sorry you had Misty or that you kept her. She's a wonderful little girl."

After several tense moments, Gracie tugged her hand

free, stood up and wandered over to the rosebushes. "I thought maybe you were sorry we got married, that you'd come back to say you'd found someone else, and to ask me for a divorce. Then I thought if you knew about Misty you'd try to take her away." She gulped back a sob. "When I saw you in the park, all I could think of was that nothing would ever be the same for Misty and me."

Dallas walked over behind her and slid his arms around her waist, turning her so she faced him.

"Things won't ever be the same, Gracie. But I hope, I pray they'll be better." He bent his head, brushed his lips against hers, and when she kissed him back he deepened it, hoping, praying that her response was meant for him, not the man she'd lost six years ago.

He tilted his head back to study her beautiful face, but she quickly buried it against his chest. So he rested his chin on her silken head, relishing their contact.

"That should tell you that I don't want a divorce, Gracie. We are married, and in my book that means forever. What we have to do now is figure out a way to make our marriage work."

"But Misty… I have to put her first, Dallas. I can't put her world on hold to help you get back yours. Don't you see? It isn't about us." Gracie eased out of his embrace. "We're adults. We can adjust, adapt. But Misty is a little girl who needs security."

"I'm not asking you to abandon Misty!" Her comments puzzled him. "Misty doesn't strike me as insecure, Gracie. She knows you'll be there. But she's not going to be content to stay locked up in the world you've created for her. Already she's made new friends, found new confidence. Isn't that what you want for her?"

"My mother died when I was four. I thought she'd gone away, left me because she didn't like me. I cried for three days before someone told me she still loved me, even though she was in Heaven."

Pain, poker hot and just as sharp, pierced his skull. Dallas gasped, grabbed his head between his hands, groaning as white-hot flashes of light flared before him.

"Dallas? What's wrong?"

He couldn't respond, couldn't do anything but try to outlast it. When the agony finally ebbed, he was too drained to stand, so he flopped down on the nearest chair.

"What happened?" Gracie asked, pushing back his hair so she could study his face.

"Did your mother die when you were four?" It was the only thing that made sense—a memory.

"What on earth does that—"

"Tell me!"

Gracie nodded. "Yes, she did."

"I think I just had a flashback, a memory of the time you told me that." The pieces were tumbling together as he saw the shadows move across her face.

She frowned, but he wouldn't let her speak. Not now. Not when he had to say what had just become so clear.

"You lost your mother and that colors your perceptions. But Misty isn't you. And I'm not your father." He dragged her hands from his shoulders, gripped them. "Our daughter is not going to have to face what you did, Gracie."

"H-how do you know?" she whispered.

"Because we are not your parents. Because I trust God to show me how to be the father that Misty needs, the husband you need." He leaned forward. "Because our daughter already knows you love her more than life."

He kissed her again with all the hope his soul could muster, then quietly left the house, his senses muddled but his mind focused on one thing—getting his family back.

"You're pushing her too high."

"No, I'm not." He didn't laugh at her fear, but he didn't stop pushing Misty on the swing, either. "The ropes are secure, Gracie. Misty's hanging on. Nothing's going to happen, so relax."

With many other families using the ranch's playground today, it was impossible for her to tell him off. Not that she would in front of Misty, anyway. But Gracie was growing weary of Dallas's determined efforts to disqualify her fears.

"You have to stop hovering, Gracie." He came over and sat down beside her. "She needs to be more independent." He called out to Misty how many steps away they were. "And the slide is ten steps behind you if you want to play there."

It was the very method Gracie had read about in the books her doctor had loaned her, the same method taught at the clinics she couldn't afford to send Misty to. But Gracie didn't practice it herself. Misty always seemed too young, too vulnerable. So she'd put off pushing her child to discover her world by herself. After all, there'd be time enough.

Dallas clearly didn't share this philosophy.

"You're not doing her any favors, you know," he

said, shifting on the old quilt she'd brought. "Emily said they should learn as much independence as quickly as possible, and that five isn't too young. She said she told you that the first day you met."

A hint of condemnation in his voice made her flush. "I've been working up to it."

"You've been avoiding it."

To avert an argument, Gracie began to rise, to go to Misty. Dallas's hand on her arm prevented that.

"You're only making her world more difficult for her if you don't prepare her properly," he said quietly. "Misty's very clever. She senses your fear and she's attributing it to herself, to a weakness she thinks you see."

"That's ridiculous."

He stared at their little girl with eyes blazing, his love obvious. "You think of her as handicapped, but she doesn't see herself that way. Not yet. Misty has all kinds of dreams and she's raring to fulfill them. Please don't get in her way."

"It's my job to protect her."

"And mine," he reminded her.

"You don't know what might happen."

"Neither do you. All we can do is instill confidence in her to handle every situation."

Gracie couldn't think of anything to rebut that so she sat still, watching as Misty gradually slowed the swing. But when she jumped off and tumbled onto the grass, Gracie bolted to her feet.

Dallas rose, too, his hand on her arm as he called out how many steps to the teeter-totter. "I'll be there in a minute." He turned to Gracie, his face earnest. "I'm her father. Please let us have some time together. After the busy week we've had, you need a break. Take it. Let her get to know herself. And me her. Without watching us all the time."

His pleading voice affected Gracie. "I'll think about it."

"Trust me, won't you?"

"I'm trying."

"I know. I appreciate it." He brushed his thumb over her lips, causing a minor earthquake in the region of her heart. "You stretch out, get a bit of color in your cheeks. Misty and I will be over there." Dallas pointed to the teeter-totter, brushed his hand against her hair, then loped across the grass toward their daughter.

Gracie sat down, knees too weak to hold her upright.

Dallas was taking over. She hadn't really absorbed the fact that he was back yet, and now watching him move Misty up and down on the beam didn't reassure her at all. In her mind she knew he was right, that she had to help Misty become more independent. But in her heart all Gracie wanted was to snuggle her precious baby close and keep her safe from all of life's troubles.

She needed Misty as much as Misty needed her.

Gracie remained seated on the blanket, watching. And while she watched, she saw her child gain confidence as Dallas encouraged her to try different things. The swing, the teeter-totter, hanging from the bars—Misty gloried in all of them, her face beaming with excitement. But when Dallas held her up so she could grasp the handle of the child's zip-line, Gracie could no longer stay silent. She got up and approached the teeter-totter.

"I think that's enough now."

"Not yet, Mommy. This is the most fun I've ever

had!" Misty hollered, then squealed with delight as Dallas let her go and she swung through the air.

Gracie tried to repress the hurt. A glance at Dallas's face told her he understood her pain, how deeply those innocent words cut, when she'd spent the past five years giving everything she had.

"Don't be upset, Gracie. She didn't mean anything by it."

She jerked her eyes away from his, scanned the playground to where Misty had just walked.

"She's talking to Rory. She's fine."

Rory and two other children Gracie didn't recognize.

"They're just being kids, joking with each other. They'll be fine."

He was right. Rory had hold of Misty's hand and was leading her toward the swings. He waited until she'd climbed into one before laying down his canes and gently pushing the swing into motion.

"Rory's mother is watching them, Gracie. They'll be fine."

Just then a woman waved her hand and smiled.

"Misty was trying to convince him to play with the dolls she brought in her backpack. Rory has a truck. Dolls and trucks don't seem to go together, but they worked it out. Kids usually do."

"I guess." Gracie fiddled with the grass, pulling the greenest spears.

"You're with her or at work all the time. Don't you ever want some time to yourself?"

"What do you mean?" Suspicion edged its way into her heart.

"I mean you have no free time. It must be difficult."

"I love Misty."

"I know that, but if I were to spend a day with her, or even an afternoon, you could go shopping, get your hair done, whatever." Dallas's voice softened. "She'd be safe with me, Gracie."

"That's what it's really about, isn't it? You're trying to steal my daughter." Her heart filled with fury and fear.

"My daughter, too, remember." He sighed, tilted his head back as if stretching out a knot in his neck. "I'm not going to kidnap her. I just want, need, time to be with her, for her to get used to me. That's all I'm asking for, Gracie."

That's all he was asking now. But what would happen when his memory returned? Dallas kept wanting more and more. What if he wanted to take Misty away with him? How would Gracie combat his parents?

"We've seen a hundred girls exactly like you. Girls claiming to be our son's wives, girlfriends, lovers. You'll say anything to collect that reward money, won't you? But our son would have told us if he'd married. He would not have left his wife alone and pregnant. So I'd advise you to go and don't come back. Or we'll have you arrested."

The memory of that big oak door slamming shut in her face still stung. Gracie jumped to her feet.

"What's wrong?"

Dallas was good at reading her. He'd probe and press until she finally admitted the truth, and that was the one thing Gracie had promised herself she'd never do. He would never know how callously they'd treated her, of their arrogant dismissal when she'd needed them so desperately. She could never tell him that his own parents had rejected her and the child she was carrying.

"Gracie?"

"You want time with her? You've got this afternoon. I'll be back in a couple of hours."

She checked one last time to be sure Misty was all right. Dallas noticed.

"She'll be fine. I'll make sure of that, Gracie, I promise." He was beside her, touching her arm. "You can trust me."

She stepped away, desperate to escape the fluttering of her heart. "I'll just tell her so she won't worry when I'm not here."

Dallas said nothing, simply stood there while Gracie explained to Misty.

"Okay, Mommy. Me and Rory are going to play for a while, then Dallas said I could have a big ice cream cone. A chocolate one."

"That sounds yummy." She hugged the tiny girl to her heart, kissed her cheek and hurriedly said goodbye. Misty was so easily willing to replace her with Dallas. The knowledge scraped her already skinned nerves.

Sympathy shone in Dallas's dark gaze. Gracie turned away from it.

"See you later," she said.

But as she drove toward the city, Gracie couldn't help wondering if this was the first of many times she'd be on her own while father and daughter enjoyed a day. Fear grabbed her at the thought of being locked out of Misty's life.

Unsure of what to do with her newfound freedom, Gracie headed for the only place in Dallas she'd ever found happiness. The arboretum.

* * *

Dallas knew he'd goofed badly when he took Misty home and found Gracie thrashing through the pool.

He'd seen her vehicle return, knew she hadn't been able to stay away, to trust him without being there in case her daughter needed her. That lack of trust had bitten deeply.

He had to keep reminding himself that he had left her for six years. Remember that she recalled every lonely night, every terror-filled moment when no one had been there to support or encourage her.

By the time Gracie climbed out of the water and pretended to listen to Misty's long-winded explanation of what they'd done that afternoon, Dallas had conquered his irritation at her unreasonable fear. Now he just wished he could wrap his arms around her.

"That's lovely, darling. I'm glad you enjoyed yourself. I guess I'd better get dinner."

"But that's the best part. Me and Dallas made pizza!" Misty glowed with excitement. "I cut up the peppers and onions and mushrooms."

"Cut?" Gracie's blue eyes turned glacial.

"She used a table knife," he said softly.

"An' I grated some of the cheese. But I cutted my hand. See?" Misty held up her bandaged knuckle for her mother's inspection. "It doesn't hurt. Not really. Cheese feels funny when you grate it."

"Does it?"

"We went on a frog hunt after that. Dallas lets me do lots of stuff, Mommy. Can we do stuff with him tomorrow?"

"We'll see."

Misty sighed, nudged him in the ribs. "That mostly means no," she said, her forehead creasing. "I don't think Mommy is very happy."

"I'm—"

"Didn't you have a good time shopping, Mommy?" She danced from one foot to the other. "Did you buy a new dress?"

"A new dress? Why? Do I need one?"

Dallas winced at the glare she shot his way.

"You always look lovely," he said sincerely, wishing he remembered more about his wife's quicksilver moods. "No matter what you wear."

"Dallas said he'll take us for real pizza sometime," Misty interjected. "To a pizza restaurant called Martini's. I thought maybe you went to get a dress for that."

"Martini's?" Gracie frowned at him. "You remembered?"

"The name." He shrugged. "It came back when we were making the pizza. It seemed important so I checked in the phone book. I guess it's still doing business."

"Yes, it is." Gracie looked away, her cheeks slightly pink.

She pretended nonchalance, but Dallas knew from her reaction there was more to it. "What else should I have remembered, Gracie?"

"We had dinner there after we were married."

"Oh." He prayed for patience. Would these black holes ever fill with memories again?

Silence stretched for a few moments.

"What did you make your pizza crust out of?"

"I borrowed some refrigerator dough from the mess

hall cook." He waited for her to comment on the lack of nutrition, but Gracie only held his gaze for several moments. Then she smiled.

"Then I guess we'd better cook it. Or you should. I'll shower while you and Misty get things ready." Gracie went into the house, leaving them on the patio.

Dallas caught the challenge in her comment. He wanted time with his daughter; she'd give it to him and watch him royally mess up.

Only Dallas didn't intend to mess up. Every time he looked at Misty he had an urge to tell the whole world, *This is my little girl.* He believed God was with him, helping him regain his life.

"Come on, Miss. We have to get dinner on." Dallas put their pizza in the oven and then showed Misty how to set the table.

"Very good!" He applauded when she'd arranged two other settings exactly like his. "Now we'll pour you a drink."

Misty dribbled a lot onto the counter but she was proud of herself for filling the glass. While they waited for the pizza to be done, they happily created a salad together.

Gracie seemed pleased at their accomplishments, until he stayed her hand when she would have stopped Misty from serving the first slice of pizza. Then her face froze, she jerked her hand away and said nothing more to him.

"Excellent service, Miss Henderson. Now mine." He held out his plate.

Misty found the edge of the plate he held out, slid the server under another piece of pizza, then carefully laid it on his plate. She glowed with pride. Dallas stared at Gracie, silently begging her to notice.

"It's wonderful pizza, honey. And the salad was scrumptious. You're a good cook." She hugged Misty until the little girl wiggled away, insisting her mother had to taste the dessert, which turned out to be an apple for each of them, polished to a high sheen.

Funny how much Dallas wished Gracie would hug him like that.

But he couldn't have been prouder of Misty's success. He cleaned up the kitchen while Gracie helped Misty prepare for bed. Twice he heard the sound of stifled yawns, proof of Misty's overtiredness. His fault.

"Can I help?" He stood in the doorway of Misty's room, noting the weary slope of Gracie's shoulders. She was running on nerves. "How about bedtime prayers?"

"I already said them. It's time for a story. I always have a story before bed, but Mommy says not tonight," Misty told him, pouting.

"Would it be okay if I sang a lullaby instead?" Dallas offered, longing to be a part of their ritual.

"Sing?" It was clear his wife had forgotten his love of music, something he'd only recently discovered himself.

"I don't have a guitar, but I think I can still carry a tune. Shove over, kiddo." At least Misty seemed excited.

Dallas thought for a moment, then began a ballad that had been in his head for the past several days. He heard a muffled sound behind him, saw Gracie rush out.

What now? Something from the past, no doubt.

He was weary of these land mines. If he could only remember.

Misty pressed him to continue, and he did. In fact,

he made it halfway through the second verse before her eyelids dropped and she sighed, snuggled into her pillow and fell fast asleep.

Dallas eased off the bed and pulled the covers up to her chin. He bent, brushed his lips against her porcelain skin.

"Good night, sweet Misty."

The night-light was already on so he left the room, and prayed for wisdom when he saw Gracie hunched over on the patio, her cheeks shiny with tears in the bright moonlight.

Chapter Six

Gracie knew the moment Dallas left Misty's room. She heard his light-footed tread, the swish of the patio door, his quick, soft inhalation before he stepped outside.

Every movement made her nerves tighter.

She'd chosen to sit in the patio swing beside the door. Dallas sat down beside her, touched her chin so she had to look at him. Her blood traitorously sang at his touch.

"What did I do wrong?"

"Nothing." She summoned a smile. "It's just... hard. You know?"

"Because you've been her world for so long and now I'm butting in and taking over."

She blinked at him in surprise.

"I'm not trying to push you out, Gracie. But we're both her parents. That's the way God created families. She needs both of us. We bring balance to her world."

"I know."

"But?"

"I saw the way she handled making the pizza and the salad, Dallas. I know I've shielded her too much."

"Misty learns so quickly. She could do so much more for herself." *If you'd let her.*

"I didn't intentionally stunt her growth, you know." Anger flared, red-hot. "I don't know why you persist in seeing me as some kind of domineering witch who cages her daughter. It isn't like that. I give her as much freedom as I can, but I also have to be mindful of her boundaries. Just because you have her doing new things doesn't change my role or make my decisions wrong."

"Gracie, I'm not criticizing you."

"It sure seems like it." The memories of his song and its promise ate at her composure, but Grace hung on, struggled to refocus on what she needed to say. "For five years I've had to gauge every decision, make sure I didn't press too hard, ease forward, with no idea if I was doing the right thing or the wrong. I've put everything on hold so that Misty can develop at her own pace. It hasn't exactly been easy and I've questioned my choices many times."

"You've done a wonderful job with her."

"I couldn't afford the extras she should have had. I did what I could but—" She bit her lip, refusing to break down now.

"Gracie, you did everything right. Look at Misty, really look at her, and you'll know that. The extras don't matter."

"They do, though," she whispered, finally accepting that Dallas could give their child far more than she ever could. "I realized she needed more, but I couldn't do anything about it until I finished my training. Then, when Elizabeth asked me to come here, I jumped at the chance, even though it meant leaving everything familiar behind. It was a way to get all the things for Misty that I couldn't provide. People who know what she needs, a place where she's safe, more time to spend with her."

All the things Dallas and his parents could give her without a second thought.

"You've made good choices."

"Have I? I'm not so sure."

Gracie thought of the nights she'd sat watching her baby, wondering if she should have gone back to his parents' house, forced them to see how much Misty resembled Dallas. His parents could have paid for anything Misty needed. Her little girl might have wanted for nothing if Gracie had only pushed them.

But what if they'd tried to take her baby? The terror of that possibility had directed every decision.

"The past is done, Gracie. We can't change it. All we have is tomorrow."

"Yes." At least until the police found his parents.

"So? Will you let her spend more time with me? Without coming back early, checking up on us, getting other people to report on me?"

Heat scorched her cheeks. Dallas knew what she'd been doing; knew but didn't seem angry.

He was trying so hard. He loved their daughter. He would never let anything hurt her.

Gracie capitulated. "Wednesday evenings. I need a couple of hours to keep up with my records. Maybe…" She swallowed hard. "Maybe you could make her dinner, put her to bed?"

"I could," he whispered, covering Gracie's hand with his. "And perhaps Sundays? Could I take her to church?"

"Church?" To learn about God—who hadn't been there when Gracie needed Him most?

"They have a class for kids her age. She'd meet new friends. It would expose her to somewhere other than the Bar None. Only for a few hours. You could come, too, if you want to make sure it's okay."

"Why church?" The pleading in Dallas's voice, the light in his eyes confused her. What had God done for him except take everything away?

"Because I want Misty to know God loves her and that He'll be with her always. That she can count on Him when you and I seem to fail her." Dallas's eyes blazed with a light Gracie didn't understand. "It's the only thing that's helped me through the darkest times. The knowledge that even if I never remember, God will still be with me and that He'll help me figure out my next step."

"I guess it would be okay," she muttered.

"Thank you." He hugged her, drawing her to him. "We'll get through this, Gracie. You and me. Together. We'll figure out how to raise our daughter the way God intended."

"I'm not real big on God," she admitted. His chest rumbled beneath her. He was laughing.

"That doesn't matter, honey," he said into her hair.

"It doesn't?" He didn't try to persuade or convince her to share his faith. That surprised her. "Why?"

"Because God is big on you. He loves you dearly and He will never, ever walk away if you ask Him for help."

A lump formed in Gracie's throat. Dallas's hand stroked over her head as she struggled to speak.

"He did walk away from me. I prayed and prayed that you would come back. But you never did. Where was God then, Dallas?"

"Right beside you." He cupped his hands against her cheeks, lifted her head so she had to meet his gaze. "God didn't leave you or abandon you, Gracie. He was there every step of the way, even when you didn't realize it." Dallas's thumb brushed over her mouth.

Gracie fought past the longing. She needed the answer to this question. "Then why didn't He change things? Why didn't He send you home?"

"I don't know, sweetheart. I only know that somehow, some way, He will bring good out of what we think is bad. If you trust no one else, trust Him."

Dallas kissed her, slowly, but with a world of feeling packed into that gentle embrace. For a moment Gracie was transported back in time to those first heady moments of marriage, when she'd believed the world was finally granting her wildest dream,

But then thunder rumbled in the distance, lightning blazed across the sky and she was back in no-man's-land, married, but not really.

She recoiled, tried to ease away from him. But Dallas didn't let her go. He captured her face again, stared into her eyes, his own clear, determined.

"I can't go back, Gracie. I can't make anything better or be the guy you remember. All I can do is be here now, do my best to care for you and our child, and pray God will heal my mind so I can be the husband and father I should be. I trust Him to do that. Can you?"

"I don't know," she answered honestly after a stretch of time. "Trust isn't something I do easily."

"You'll wait and see? Is that it?" Dallas smiled sadly, traced her eyebrows, the line of her nose, the fullness of her top lip and the jut of her chin.

"I guess." She wished he'd kiss her again. When he did that all the fears and worries melted and she could only remember how much she'd loved him, how much hope had built up inside during those eight short days of marriage, how the fear that no one would ever love her had finally shriveled and died. "I'll try."

"Then we'll go with that. But remember one thing, Gracie." His arms fell away. All that held her now was the sheen in his eyes. "God won't push His way into your life. Either you accept that He is who He says He is, that He has His own reasons for doing things, or you don't."

She wasn't sure she understood exactly what Dallas was saying. She knew he wanted to share her parenting role, and she was prepared to allow that.

But the God he was talking about wasn't a concept she understood.

God had taken her husband, abandoned her and her baby when they most needed Him. How could she depend on Him now?

"Tomorrow is Sunday. I'll be here at nine. We can all go together. Okay?"

Gracie was going to refuse, but suddenly changed her mind. Her job as Misty's mother meant she had a duty to check out the church.

"I'll be ready."

Dallas couldn't hide his surprise as he held out a hand, drew her up beside him.

"Thank you," he said simply.

"You're welcome."

He studied her for a long time. Gracie could feel the heat from his hand on hers, the awareness that rippled through her body whenever he touched her.

Attraction hummed between them now, impossible to ignore. Twice as powerful because Misty wasn't there to buffer it.

"I know why I married you, Gracie," Dallas whispered, his voice so soft she barely heard it over the thunder.

"You do?" She froze, unable to move when his fingers tangled with hers, when his other hand slipped over her hair, down the nape of her neck and across her shoulder. A sliver of hope crept in, twined around her heart.

He'd remembered something.

"I married you because you're so full of love." His hand curved over the very top of her arm. He held it there, squeezed gently, as if to impress her with his words. "It's tucked away in your heart, waiting to rush out."

Because she didn't know how to answer that, Gracie stood very still.

"You've been hurt, so you pushed it out of sight. But it's still there. Waiting."

She couldn't say anything when Dallas stared into her eyes like that.

"I envy the man you married, Gracie."

"But—"

"I envy him because you loved him more than life. He was a fool to leave." Dallas bent his head, pressed one hard kiss against her lips, then drew back. "Good night."

He turned, walked to the gate and quietly let himself out. Gracie lifted a hand, touched her mouth.

"Good night," she whispered.

The man who'd just left wasn't the man she'd married. But he was someone her heart recognized.

Dallas loved the little church with its friendly faces and welcoming feeling. He made a note to thank Elizabeth for directing him to it. The building was unpretentious, the piano rudimentary, the congregation small. But that didn't matter.

He loved sitting in the pew with his wife and daughter, singing praises to the One who was his Lord. Had he done this before? Gone to church with Gracie?

Dallas had no answers. But as the minister preached a Mother's Day sermon, Dallas soaked in the words. And translated them to fit his personal situation.

God expected him to love the way a real husband, a real father would. Only then could he finally be healed. If Dallas couldn't make progress in those relationships he would be no better than a friend helping Gracie, a doting uncle to his daughter. The thought chilled him.

Uncles, friends—they were simply onlookers. They visited, shared a few moments, then returned to their own lives. To be needed, to be wanted, to have his daughter see him as an integral part of her life, not a visitor—that was Dallas's goal. He ached for Gracie to talk to him as if his opinion mattered, as if she valued his input. He wanted to be part of their lives, a part they couldn't do without.

Too quickly the service came to an end.

"Hi, I'm Mike," the minister said, shaking their hands at the door. "Is this Misty?"

"Yes. I'm Dallas. And this is Gracie. We're her parents."

"Pleased to meet you. I've heard all about Misty from Rory." The minister bent down to her. "I hear you have quite a rapport with horses. Rory said you got a wild one to eat out of your hand."

Beside Dallas Gracie went rigid. The smile stayed pasted on her face, but he knew she was not pleased.

"Rory an' me like horses," Misty said happily. "Dallas is going to teach me to ride."

Gracie pinned him with a hard glare.

"It was a great sermon." Dallas struggled to breach the conversation gap.

"Thanks." Mike handed Gracie a small pot with a daisy. "Happy Mother's Day, Mrs. Henderson." He shook her hand. "I was wondering if perhaps Misty would like to join our children's choir."

Misty perked up at this, began asking a hundred questions. Satisfied that Rory was a member, she turned to her mother.

"Can I sing in the choir?" she demanded.

"She has quite a good voice," Dallas murmured, hoping Gracie wouldn't nix the idea because of him. "We were singing yesterday. Emily lent me her guitar. Misty stayed on key the entire time."

"I see." Gracie's pretty lips tightened. "We'll talk about it later. Thank you, Reverend."

"Call me Mike." He grinned. "We have a ladies' Bible study starting next week, Mrs. Henderson. In case you're interested."

"We'll see."

They left the church, Misty swinging between them, chattering excitedly about the choir. Gracie seemed less enthused.

"I thought maybe we could go to Martini's," Dallas murmured as they settled in the truck. "For Mother's Day."

"Surprise!" Misty squealed from the backseat, wiggling so hard Dallas wondered if the restraint would hold. "I got you a present, too, but you can't have it yet. Dallas said that's not part of the plan."

"The plan. I see." The way Gracie said it bugged him.

"It's not a state secret. We wanted to surprise you, that's all," Dallas told her.

"You have. By all means, let's go to Martini's."

An inauspicious beginning, but thanks to Misty's unbridled enthusiasm, the meal turned out better than he'd expected. They stopped by the arboretum after, where Gracie opened her gifts—a collage of tiny foam tiles that Misty had made into a picture, and a silver necklace with a locket from him. Elizabeth had helped there, too.

Gracie enthused over the picture, but only thanked him quietly for the locket. Dallas told himself not to feel hurt, but his heart didn't listen.

"Look inside," Misty ordered as she danced across the grass. "It's a picture of me on the swing. Dallas took it with Elizabeth's camera. We put it inside."

"You look very lovely, dear."

She seemed about to return it to its box. Dallas rested his hand on hers. "Can I put it on for you, Gracie?"

She studied him, her eyes shrouded. Finally, she nodded.

He lifted the delicate chain, undid the clasp and set the chain around her neck. His fingers grazed her skin, lighting a fire inside him, but Dallas tamped it down, heeding the voice inside.

Go slow.

"Thank you."

"Thank you for being a wonderful mother, Gracie."

She frowned, then noticed Misty had wandered away from them and was now tumbling happily across the grass.

"Misty, be—"

Dallas touched her lips with his finger. "Don't."

Gracie knocked his hand away. "Do not tell me how to care for my daughter."

So they were back to that again.

"She's free," he whispered, trying to help Gracie see. "For a few moments in her very careful world, she's free to let go and play. Don't ruin it."

Gracie opened her lips to say something, thought better of it and studied him instead. Dallas held still under that probing scrutiny, longing to gather her into his arms and soothe away her fears as easily as Misty had shed her own.

A squeal interrupted the moment.

"He's been watching me for a long time." Misty sat perfectly still, her head tilted to one side as she listened to the dog panting contentedly beside her.

"Where did that dog come from?" Dallas asked.

"Maybe we should—"

"He's a beautiful dog, Miss. Why don't you talk to him?"

"Hello, dog."

The dog woofed a quiet greeting. One paw touched her skirt, which was flounced out around her on the grass. Misty's lips moved soundlessly, then she reached out a hand. The dog's haunches twitched but he stood perfectly still as she brushed her fingers over his side, stroking the red-gold fur as she absorbed every detail.

"Dallas, stop staring at that thing and do something." Gracie grabbed his hand.

"Wait." Dallas wasn't sure why, he only knew his daughter was in the midst of a discovery, and he didn't want to ruin it. The dog wasn't threatening or uncomfortable. In fact, he seemed to have built an immediate connection with the little girl.

"You're very big," Misty whispered, her hands stilling as the dog lay down beside her, pushed his head under her hand. "Your head is big." She moved her fingers.

When the chubby digits moved too near the animal's teeth, Gracie gasped, but Dallas held on to her hand.

"Give her a minute."

"You have such nice fur. When I get my Seeing Eye dog, I hope he's like you. You're strong but nice." Misty murmured little comments, all the while stroking the dog until he finally stretched forward and swiped her face with his tongue. She giggled. "Mommy, look at this dog. He's kissing me."

Gracie was speechless.

"We're looking, sweetie. He sure does like you," Dallas called.

Misty pushed the furry head away but the dog was not to be moved. He thrust his muzzle into her lap and closed his eyes.

Misty's delicate fingers eased over the animal, memorizing the silken ears, the long neck, the beautifully combed hair. The dog was obviously well cared for.

"I wonder who he belongs to." Dallas scanned the park. It took a minute before he saw a little girl in a wheelchair. She was searching left and right, calling something. "Misty, I think someone is looking for that dog. I'm going to tell her he's here. Okay? Mommy will be here, on the bench. Fifteen steps," he said.

"Okay."

"Dallas, you can't leave her with him. What if—"

"If he wants to leave, don't hang on to him, okay, Misty? He might hear his owner and know he has to go back."

"Okay."

"She'll be all right," he whispered to Gracie. "The dog is trained. Look at his collar. Those tags are specific to animals trained by the Tarvin Academy. It uses behavior modified animals for special-needs kids."

Gracie frowned. "Are you sure?"

"Yes." He didn't know why he knew that, but Dallas was certain of the dog's integrity. He squeezed Gracie's hand, then loped across the grass to the young girl in the wheelchair. "Did you lose your dog?"

The child blinked, stared at him.

"An Irish setter?"

"Y-yes." She sniffed. "You know Rusty?"

"He's lying with my little girl on the grass. She's blind and he's letting her pet him." He explained that he didn't want to startle the dog, asked if they'd come with him. The little girl nodded, pulled out a leash.

"How did Rusty get away?" Dallas asked.

"He likes to run. I let him off the leash. He went twice, but the third time he didn't come back." She let go of the button on her chair, paused. "Did your little girl have ice cream?"

"A big cone. She spilled it all over her dress."

"Rusty loves the smell of ice cream," the child's

mother explained. "It's the only thing that seems to make him disobey."

"You should tell Tarvin. I'm sure they have a procedure for curing that. How long have you had Rusty?"

"Three months. How did you know he was from Tarvin?"

"His collar." It wasn't true. Something inside Dallas had recognized the animal's actions, the specific sloping of the skull that signaled the dog's acquiescence. The way the setter angled his head, held his stance—he knew those moves, knew the animal had been trained at the Tarvin facility.

But how did he know it?

"Stay, Rusty," the little girl called as they got closer to Misty. She wheeled her chair as near as she could and the two began chatting.

"Gracie, this is…" Dallas paused. He didn't know their names.

"Sarah Frank and that's Amanda, my daughter."

"It's nice to meet you."

They spent a few minutes talking. Dallas knew Gracie wouldn't linger long. She hid it, but she was still steaming. At him.

"I think it's time we headed home," Dallas said a short time later. "Thanks so much for sharing Rusty."

Misty reluctantly said goodbye to her new friends, then grasped Dallas's hand as they headed back to the truck. Halfway there she stumbled, and he scooped her up in his arms, set her on his shoulders.

She was asleep when they reached the truck. He tucked her in her seat, did up the belts, waited while Gracie checked his work. Once they were on the road, he opened his mouth a couple of times to ask her what was wrong, but decided it would be safer to let her negotiate traffic first.

At Gracie's house, Dallas undid Misty's belt and carried her inside. In a few minutes Gracie had her out of her sticky dress and tucked into bed for a nap.

She made sure everything was in its place before leading Dallas from the room.

"I suppose I should go," he said.

"Oh, no you don't." She picked up the baby monitor, grabbed his arm and pulled. "You have a few things to explain, Dallas."

Dallas didn't need anyone to explain that they were about to have their first argument.

Chapter Seven

"How dare you, Dallas Henderson!"

Gracie was so mad. It didn't help that he sat there staring at her as if she'd asked him to pass the mustard.

"How dare I what? What did I do?"

"Misty fed that wild stallion that just came in. You actually let her get within reach of his teeth, didn't you?"

Dallas couldn't lie so he stayed silent.

"He's a wild animal, Dallas."

"He's not wild. He let me sit on him."

So he'd been working with the new horse when she wasn't there. Though it galled her, Gracie knew she couldn't argue over that. He was an employee of the ranch, after all. And he did know about gentling animals.

But Misty didn't.

"He could have bitten her. I haven't given him all his shots yet. Who knows what he carries?"

"Gracie, you know animals. Did Patch look that dangerous to you?"

Patch. He'd already named the black-and-white pinto. Somehow that made her angrier.

"Until we came here she'd never been near a horse. She doesn't know how to handle a tame one, let alone a wild thing that's barely been ridden. How could you deliberately put her in danger?"

"I'm her father." Dallas stood, his own color rising. "I would never endanger Misty, no matter what you think."

"Well, you did."

"No. I taught her how to hold the grass so he could sniff it and then eat it. I taught her that not all things are bad or dangerous, that sometimes creatures just need a little love. I'm trying to teach her not to be afraid."

"I'll teach my daughter those things. In my own time. My way," Gracie snapped. She was losing control of everything. And she hated it.

"Really? How will you teach her not to be afraid when you're scared of everything? I have a right to spend time teaching her things. You agreed to that."

"Not with the horses. I don't want her near the horses."

She shouldn't have said that.

Gracie knew the moment the words left her lips that she'd opened a crevasse between them.

"Why? What's wrong with horses?" He was standing too close, pressing for answers she didn't want to give. "Patch isn't wild. He may have run loose for a while but he was broken. He's not dangerous."

"I'm setting the ground rules here. And I say no horses, Dallas. I mean it."

"This is a ranch. Horses are a part of it." He frowned in confusion. "How can she possibly stay away from them? All the kids will be starting riding lessons next week."

"Misty won't be among them."

"What?" He couldn't believe she would refuse, but her glacial glare wasn't melting. "Why shouldn't she join the rest of the kids?"

Why did he refuse to see? Gracie swallowed. She'd have to spell it out for him.

"Misty is blind, Dallas. She can't direct a horse, can't stop it if it goes out of control. The horses are too big for her. If she falls she'll hurt herself. I won't allow it."

Dallas dragged a hand through his hair, his brows lowered. "Do you hear yourself, Gracie? You're denying her the chance to blend in with the other kids doing something she could enjoy. Why?"

"They don't have the same disabilities," she snapped stubbornly.

"Some of them do." He lifted her chin, frowned at what he saw in her eyes. "What's really going on? You said you brought her here to help her become more independent."

"There's not a situation in the real world in which she'd have to ride a horse. There's no need to take the risk."

"There's every need." Dallas glared at her. "Did you see her with Rusty this afternoon? She built a rapport with that dog so fast it was amazing. I've never seen anything like that. She did the same with Patch. She has the ability to understand animals and they understand her."

"Like you do, you mean?" Gracie winced at the scathing note in her voice. But she could not stop the words from coming. "Are you sure you're not projecting your abilities onto Misty, Dallas?"

"Are you sure you're not projecting your fears?"

"How dare you?" Outraged, she jumped up from her chair.

"I dare because I love that child and I want her to experience everything in life that she can. There's always a chance something could hurt her, Gracie. But there's a bigger change she'll be enriched."

Anger took over. "You are so naive. You haven't changed at all, Dallas. You waltz through life expecting that everything will go the way you want it to." She glared at him, bitterness welling up. "Well, life isn't like that. Things happen that shouldn't and some of us have to pick up the pieces. I protect what I love. I don't risk it."

"That's not fair!" Dallas was angry, too. He glared at her. "I didn't deliberately abandon you, Gracie, so stop playing the martyr."

The angry words chafed her and she opened her mouth to retort.

"Why are you arguing, Mommy?"

Gracie stifled a groan.

"Is it because I did something wrong?" Misty's voice echoed her doubts.

Dallas shot her a look that plainly said, *See?* He hunched down in front of his daughter, hugged her close.

"No, Misty. You didn't do anything wrong. Not at all. We were just discussing things and we got a bit angry. But that's okay. Lots of people disagree. We'll talk it over and we'll come to an understanding."

"But you were arguing about me." Misty held still for a moment, then shifted out of his grasp. She walked to her mother, touched her hand. "Mommy?"

"Everything's fine, honey."

"I know you told me not to go near the horses, but Dallas said it was okay. He said we'd just stop and say hello."

Gracie's face turned thunder-dark. Mindful of Misty, Dallas drew his wife aside.

"Gracie, we both know Elizabeth can afford to have a riding school here because she doesn't have to buy every horse. Some are problem horses whose owners donated them, some are wild. I think Patch is different."

"Elizabeth said Patch wandered onto the ranch and wouldn't leave. She tried to find his owner, but no one responded." Her blue eyes darkened.

"Sometimes when a ranch fails, the owner releases the horses to fend for themselves." Dallas nodded. "I think that's what happened to Patch."

"He chose us? Is that what you're saying?"

"Maybe. Patch wants to be with people, that's why he doesn't leave when the gate is open. Haven't you noticed? There are lots of signs that he knows what's expected of him, signs that tell me he simply lost his way for a while. He's happy here. I can tell because he lets me sit on him."

"Patch isn't a bad horse, Mommy. Rory told me he kicked part of the fence down, but that wasn't because he's bad. Patch hurts inside."

Gracie frowned. "How do you know?"

"He told me."

"How did he tell you, honey?" She watched the heart-shaped face for an answer that would explain the certainty in Misty's solemn voice. "Did Dallas tell you Patch hurts inside?"

"No. Dallas told me to listen to him, so I did. Then… I just knew it. At first Patch was afraid I'd hurt him, like some other kids had, and he was scared to take the grass from me. But after a while he knew I wouldn't."

Dallas had given her much the same explanation six years ago when she'd asked him how he got the animals to trust him. Gracie hadn't understood it then, didn't now.

The doorbell interrupted their discussion.

One of the ranch hands stood at the door.

"Can you come, Dr. Henderson? That colt—it's not acting right."

"Yes, okay." She glanced at Dallas. "Could you stay with her?"

"No. I want to come with you, Mommy."

Gracie tried to dissuade her, but Misty was adamant.

"Dallas can come with us, can't he? We could all go together."

Seeing the urgency on the hand's face, Gracie finally gave in. As they walked toward the main barn, Misty would dart ahead a few steps, then suddenly turn around and come back, clinging tightly to Gracie's hand. On one of her forays ahead, Dallas spoke.

"She's scared," he said softly. "Our voices must have woken her and now she's afraid. I'm sorry. I never meant for that to happen."

Gracie had to tell him. "My father broke horses to pay for his schooling. He loved riding and tried to teach me when I was very young." She gulped, forced out the words. "I fell off a horse when I was three. Actually, it dragged me awhile before my dad caught it. I broke my arm. I was terrified. I guess that's stayed with me. I don't want Misty to go through what I did."

"You don't seem afraid when you're with the horses," Dallas murmured.

He placed his hand on her arm, drew her to a halt. His dark eyes searched her face, then he said quietly, "You're not three anymore. Isn't it time you conquered that fear, Gracie?"

She didn't answer. But as she worked with the colt, dropped medicine into its mouth and smoothed it down his throat, his words would not be silenced. And when Dallas led Misty into the stall near the colt, to touch it and let it lick her fingers, her tinkle of laughter, the knowing way she fondled the baby animal, brought up a question Gracie couldn't ignore.

Was fear the legacy she was passing on to her daughter?

"I don't want to go to church without you, Mommy."

Misty's whiny voice made Dallas pause on the doorstep. It had been the same all week. His daughter steadfastly refused to do anything with him unless her mother was present.

His fault.

He'd caused the argument, pushed too hard and stirred up both Gracie's and Misty's insecurities. Now he was trying to make up.

"Good morning." Dallas tapped on the screen door frame, let himself inside at Gracie's call. "Isn't it a gorgeous day today?"

"It's raining," Misty told him with a frown.

"I know. Only a shower. Besides, rain is good. It gives the land a drink, helps make the grass green so the cows can have a good lunch, and lets the horses have a break from all the bugs. We like rain."

"You're silly." She returned his hug. "I'm cleaning the kitchen while Mommy gets ready."

"Good for you." So Gracie had consented to come to church again. "Your choir is singing today, isn't it?"

"Good morning, Dallas." Gracie was so lovely his heart ached to be the one she smiled for, the one who made her laugh. He wanted to see her eyes widen the way they had the evening he'd kissed her. He wanted the right to stay here with her and Misty, not to be sent away at night.

"I like being married to you, Dallas."

The words popped up from a hidden ravine in his mind. He waited, hoping, but nothing more happened.

Would it ever?

"Why doesn't he answer me, Mommy?"

Dallas snapped back to reality.

"Sorry, Miss. I fell asleep for a minute. All that swimming with you two yesterday wore me out. What did you say?"

"I put all the dishes in the sink. Can you help me put on my dress now?"

"I can do that, sweetie." Gracie stepped forward.

"No. I want Dallas to help me."

He walked to Gracie and brushed his lips over hers.

"What was that for?"

"You. You look very beautiful."

"Thank you." She touched a hand to her mouth.

"Come on, Dallas. If you keep kissing Mommy we'll be late."

Gracie blushed. Dallas grinned, kissed her once more, then hurried after his daughter.

"How'd you know we were kissing?" he asked, curious about her ability to pick up on certain things.

"I just did," Misty told him, wiggling out of her robe. "I always know when you're kissing Mommy."

"I see." Apparently his daughter was more intuitive than he'd realized. "What did you want to talk to me about, Miss?"

"Can you close the door? Mommy's listening and this is a secret."

"Okay." He saw Gracie standing in the hall. She'd heard every word. Carefully, he closed the door. "How did you know Mommy was listening?"

"I could hear her. I always can." She slid her hand over the bed, found her dress. "I need help to put this on. Please."

"It sure has a lot of buttons." Dallas fumbled as he tried to ease the tiny pearl buttons from their loops. "There."

He slipped the dress over her head, helped her stick her arms through the sleeves, then began the arduous process of rebuttoning the pretty blue garment.

"What's the secret, Miss?" Dallas liked calling her that. It was their special name. It made Misty feel grown-up and important, and it made him feel they had a special bond between them. "Is it about Rory?"

"No. It's about Mommy. Is she sad, Dallas?"

He hesitated briefly. "Why do you ask, sweetheart?"

"Mommy had another bad dream last night. She was crying and calling your name. She kept asking God why."

"Does she have a lot of bad dreams?" He knew he shouldn't be asking Misty questions about Gracie, but Dallas was hungry for details about his wife, of what she was thinking and the past she wouldn't share with him.

"I think it's always the same one. She says she's sorry to her daddy, asks you to come back, and then cries at God." Misty frowned. "I don't like it."

"People have bad dreams sometimes, Miss. But if you get scared or worried about it, all you have to do is ask God to help and He will. He's just waiting to help."

"Always?"

"Always. No matter what."

"Maybe you better tell Mommy that."

"Maybe I will." While they had this moment, he decided to press further. He needed to figure out the contortions of Misty's mind, too. "Why wouldn't you go to the river with me yesterday? The other kids went with their parents."

"I know. Rory told me." Misty slid her feet into her white sandals, then held up one leg, waiting for him to fasten the buckles. "I wanted to go," she admitted softly. "But sometimes when I go with you Mommy gets sad. I don't want her to be sad."

Torn between parents.

It was not the way Dallas envisioned life with his daughter. He did up the second sandal before tugging her into his arms. No matter how long it took he would win Gracie over, and he would do it without hurting Misty.

"I don't want her to be sad, either, sweetheart. Let's try to cheer her up today."

"Okay. I'll sing my very bestest. What will you do?"

"I'll think of something."

And he did. By the time church was over, the rain had stopped and Dallas had it all planned.

And for once Gracie went along with his plans without comment.

They ate takeout at a picnic table in the park, followed by a game of catch, at which Misty excelled. Then he suggested a visit to the local animal shelter. The place was filled with strange sounds that had Misty confused and disoriented for a little while, until he took her around the room, explaining as they went. Misty adapted quickly and was soon seated on a rug playing with three cats.

At first Gracie objected. Dallas was ready for that.

"They've all had their shots. None of them have been labeled dangerous. Let her explore, please?"

At last Gracie relented. Several times she issued a warning to Misty to be careful, or pushed her out of the way of a wary paw. Each time Misty recoiled fearfully and Dallas had to coax her back, urging her to move slowly.

"If I'd known, I'd have brought her a change of clothes." Gracie grimaced as a kitten's paws snagged another thread in Misty's pretty dress.

"I'm sorry." Dallas wondered how long she'd saved to buy Misty the dress, and reprimanded himself for his stupidity. "I'll get her another one."

"The dress doesn't matter, Dallas." Gracie smiled as he soothed the puppy Misty had passed over in favor of the kittens. "You used to do that with our dog on the farm."

"Did I?" Now she was ready to talk about the past?

"Uh-huh. Durham was a crotchety thing, usually wouldn't let anyone but us near him. But he'd almost crawl on his belly to you, waiting for your touch."

"What a strange name for a dog."

Misty's squeak of surprise had Gracie jumping to her feet. "Misty, watch—"

Dallas intervened.

"Take it easy, Miss. The mother cat wants her babies now. Let them go and she'll back off."

"They're so soft. Like the sweater Mommy has." Misty released the kittens, rubbed her arm where a tiny scratch grew red against her white skin. "What else is here?"

Dallas watched while the attendant applied antiseptic to her arm before carrying the cats from the room. She returned with something new.

"There's a gerbil in a cage behind you," Dallas stated. "Three steps back and four away from us."

"What's a gerbil?"

While he explained, Misty followed his directions. Dallas smiled as her nimble fingers played with the lock of the cage, figuring out how to open it.

"Hold your body in front so he can't get out, then reach in and gather him into your hands. Hang on, though. We'll have a horrible job catching him if he gets away. Gerbils are fast. And sneaky."

"He has funny feet." Misty huddled over the squirming bundle, which quickly settled in her lap.

"You two are so much alike," Gracie murmured.

"She might have my way with animals, but she's also got your touch. She knows exactly how to hold it. Look."

While Gracie watched her daughter, Dallas watched Gracie, relishing her pure clear skin, the sheen of her blue eyes, the way her delicate ankles peeked beneath the hem of her skirt. A rush of pride surged through him.

A gorgeous wife, a beautiful daughter.

So why couldn't he remember?

"It's getting late. I think we should go."

He blinked, returning to reality. "You're right. We'll have to wait for the attendant to come back, though."

Gracie peered at him with those wise eyes. "Thank you," she said quietly.

"For what?"

"I know what you were doing, Dallas. I can see how quickly she adapts to new surroundings. I saw how she lost her confidence when I interfered. I get it, okay?"

"I wasn't trying to hurt you," he murmured, touching her cheek. "I only want the best for Misty."

"I know."

With the animals returned to their homes and Misty tidied up, they walked back to the truck.

"How about an ice cream?"

"Yes!"

"Only if we eat it outside," Gracie agreed. "I don't want my truck full of sticky fingers."

They were halfway through the door of the ice cream shop when it hit him.

"It's melting too fast. Look at me, Dallas." Gracie laughed up at him, her face a blend of strawberry-pink, pistachio-green and Dutch chocolate. "How do you like being married to a clown?"

"I like it quite a lot," he said, kissing her.

"Dallas?" The fingers pressing into his arm chased away the memory. "What's wrong?"

"Nothing." He struggled to catch the images, extend them, but they dissipated in the warm afternoon.

"You remembered something. What was it?"

"You. With your face plastered in ice cream." It had been Gracie, but the giggles, the twinkling eyes, the joy filling her voice—that had been a different person.

"Strawberry here." He touched her nose. "Pistachio here." Her cheek. "And chocolate right here." His fingers lingered against her chin. "You were laughing."

She studied him for several seconds before her blue eyes got very shiny and she turned away.

"Misty's waiting."

She missed him. Dallas was sure of it. That glimmer of sadness… Gracie missed her husband.

The knowledge erupted inside him in a burst of joy and triumph. For the first time, he actually felt wanted. It was just one memory, but maybe—

"What kind of ice cream can I have?" Misty was asking.

He read every label so she could choose her favorite. Then he ordered gigantic cones for himself and Gracie, and led his ladies outside to an unoccupied picnic table.

"For you, madam," he said, bowing at the waist as he handed Gracie the triple scoop.

"I can't eat all this," she said, but her eyes sparkled as she noticed the flavors he'd chosen. "It's going to drip all over me. My dress will be green and pink and brown."

"Sorry," he murmured.

But he wasn't sorry. Not at all.

Chapter Eight

Dallas was back.

Somehow Gracie hadn't expected that shared parenthood would involve so much togetherness. But lately every time she turned around he was nearby. Watching her. Touching her.

"I need the socks with the teddy bears on them, Dallas," Misty was saying. "These aren't the right ones."

"How do you know?"

"Because I can feel the ball at the back. They're not Sunday socks."

Dallas was a terrific father. Patient, gentle, encouraging—maybe too encouraging, but Misty wasn't suffering. He didn't wait to be asked to do something. The nights he sat with Misty, the house was clean and tidy when Gracie got home. He'd taken to mowing the grass, cleaning the pool. Even weeding her flower beds, something Gracie quickly put an end to. Dallas was great with animals, but flowers were not his forte.

"That's not the way to tie a dress," Gracie said.

"Well, it's my way."

Gracie chuckled. Dallas had a way of putting his touch on everything. Their toaster had been replaced with one Misty could manage on her own. The cabinets all had tags Misty used to identify what was where. Daily her little girl grew more independent. And that was good.

Not easy. Never easy to watch your baby tumble, but so wonderful to watch her pick herself up and try again.

Gracie could almost let go of the fear.

But then Elizabeth would call them into her office with a progress report on their search for Dallas's parents. What would happen when they returned?

This morning Gracie caught herself wondering how she and Misty would manage when Dallas left. He had become an integral part of their lives now. She was beginning to depend on him, to ask his opinion.

Regrets. Gracie couldn't stem them. She wished Dallas had been there to see Misty when she first smiled, took her first step; to share that earthshaking moment when she'd said her first words. Gracie ached, knowing those precious times could never be recaptured.

Which was why she'd decided to allow him to spend Sunday afternoons alone with Misty. He was right—they needed time together, and Gracie could no longer deny him those few precious hours. This past Sunday she'd deliberately stayed away, though it had been hard.

To combat her loneliness, Gracie had decided to join the ladies' Bible study Pastor Mike had told her about.

"Come on, you two. It's getting late," she said now.

Misty came laughing into the kitchen, one shoe on one shoe off. Dallas quickly followed, hair ruffled, dark eyes glowing with love.

Gracie lifted her daughter onto a chair. "Let's get this shoe on."

"My job, Mommy." Dallas drew her hands away, planted a kiss on her lips, then bent over Misty's shoes.

"Why are you always kissing Mommy, Dallas?"

Gracie gulped, saw his hands freeze on the silver buckles.

"Because I like to."

"Does she like it?"

Dallas winked at Gracie, his grin stretching wide. "Uh, I think you'll have to ask her that. In private," he warned, when Misty's pink lips popped open.

"Why?"

"Because it's personal. Maybe your mommy doesn't want me to know she likes me kissing her." He fastened the last buckle, then straightened, grasped Gracie's shoulders. "I think I should check it out for myself," he murmured.

She didn't get her protest out before his lips touched hers. By then it was too late. All common sense left her in a rush.

"That's a long time to kiss her. She must know by now," Misty squeaked.

Gracie smothered a laugh.

"You'd think so, wouldn't you?"

"Well, are you finished? Are we going now?"

"Yes, we are. Don't forget your backpack, Miss. You'll need it later." Dallas waited until Missy had skipped from the room. "You're sure you don't want to come, Gracie? You might like it."

"You always come back filthy. I'm quite sure I wouldn't like it at all." She slipped out of his arms, grabbed her handbag. "Besides, I'm going to be busy this afternoon. I'll just drop you off and pick you up later."

"You can't work all the time. Why don't you take a break by the pool? I'll serve you lunch before we go if you want."

"No, thanks." She almost laughed at the curious gleam in his eye.

"Care to share?"

"No, thanks."

He'd gloat. Dallas had been talking about God ever since she'd found him. If he knew she was going to a Bible study class he'd be exultant, and Gracie didn't want that. She needed to understand some things, figure out if she could trust God again before she talked about it with Dallas.

"Hmm, secrets, huh? Okay then. Ready?" He held out his hand and she took it.

She wasn't ready to completely trust her husband. Not yet. But she was beginning to learn

"We had hamburgers and fries and a sundae, and I went for a ride on a pony."

"What?"

"A toy pony." Dallas nipped that outburst in the bud but it was clear Gracie was upset.

"Did you ever have a sundae on Sunday, Mommy?"

"Not for a while. Let's get you into the bathtub now."

"But my toy! I want to play with Dallas and my toy."

"First we need to clean you up. Then dinner. Then bed."

"I don't want bed. I want to play with Dallas."

"I can do it, Gracie."

She shot him a look. "Yes, you can. And you should." She turned her back on him and headed for the pool area.

Dallas teased and cajoled until Misty was tucked up in bed, eyes drooping closed as he sang her to sleep.

"Sweet dreams, darling." He kissed her, checked to be sure everything she might trip on was off the floor, then left the room, drawing the door almost closed. The monitor was gone. Gracie must have it.

Gracie.

A picture of her pinched face came to him. The way she'd sat perched behind the wheel, waiting for them… Something was wrong.

He opened the French door and stepped onto the patio.

Gracie was not in the pool. She was seated on a chair.

"I'm really sorry it took us so long, Gracie. Misty was having such a good time and I hated to tear her away—"

"Of course she was having a good time," she said quietly, visibly summoning her patience. "You make sure of that, stuff her with all the foods her ogre mother won't let her have, treat her to toys and rides, anything her heart desires."

"It wasn't *anything*." He bristled, trying not to sound defensive.

"Did you tell her no even once, Dallas?"

He hadn't.

"Why should I feel guilty for that? I missed the last five years, Gracie."

"So now you're making up for them? And then what?" A tear dangled from her lashes, then plopped onto her thin cheek. "What am I supposed to do when you go, Dallas?"

"When I go?" Cold hard fear balled up inside him. She was sending him away? "I'm not leaving just because you're jealous, Gracie."

"Jealous?" She stared at him as if dazed. "Is that what you think?" She shook her head, strands of bright hair grazing her lips. "I am not jealous of you, Dallas. I'm concerned about Misty. What will happen when you leave here and there isn't someone to make a fuss over her all the time, to give her whatever she demands? How will she understand that I can't do that?"

He didn't get this. "You don't want me to buy her ice cream?"

"I don't want you to play weekend daddy whenever I'm not around. I don't want you to make her think that I'm the bad parent and you're the good one." Tears littered her cheeks now.

Dallas found a chair, sank into it.

"I just want her to love me," he whispered.

"Misty does love you, Dallas. She thinks you're superhuman, that you can do anything. You don't have to buy her love with a new present every time she asks for something." Gracie leaned forward, her face strained, white. "Maybe I do try too hard to keep her safe, but you're making it worse. You swoop in and suddenly Misty doesn't have any rules she has to obey. Then you bring her back here and I'm the disciplinarian and she hates me."

Dallas saw himself through Gracie's eyes. Dazzling Misty; laying a guilt trip on Gracie so she'd let go her controls; learning braille so he could impress his wife and daughter with his brilliance; encouraging Misty to try new things.

"She's a little girl, Dallas. One who wants to love and be loved, just like every other child. She needs parents who provide love and stability and boundaries. She has to learn that the world won't revolve around her."

In other words, stop trying to impress her and start acting like a father.

"I'm sorry, Gracie," he exclaimed, humbled by her wisdom. "I didn't mean to bowl her over. It's just—"

She smiled.

"I know. You love her. I do, too. But when you leave, I don't want her to feel abandoned."

"Gracie, honey…" He knelt in front of her. "I promise you that Misty will never feel abandoned by me. But you should know that I'm not leaving. For as long as you are here, I will be, too. If Elizabeth fires me, I'll get a job in Dallas, but I will not leave you. Do you understand?"

"But—"

He shook his head, placed his hand over her lips.

"Never. I promise."

"You can't promise that, Dallas. You don't know the future."

He gathered her hands in his, threaded their fingers together.

"I know that I made a vow to you and to God to love you until death parted us. I will honor that vow, Gracie. For as long as I live I will honor our marriage commitment. Nothing, no matter what it is, will make me leave this ranch until you ask me to go."

He saw the doubt filling her eyes, knew she believed he was only saying the words.

"But your memory…"

"Doesn't matter. I won't break that promise." He rose, drew her into his arms, wanting, needing to seal this promise in a way she couldn't forget.

"I don't think we should—"

"I do." He brushed his lips against her forehead, slid them to her earlobe. "I really do," he said, nuzzling her neck.

"Dallas, I—"

"I really, really do," he whispered one last time. Then he stopped her from saying anything more.

Even if his mind didn't remember Gracie, his heart did. Remembered the way her arms looped around his neck, the way her fingers combed through his hair, reveling in their love. His heart remembered that soft sweet sigh she made when the kiss was over, the way she leaned against him, let him bear her weight, if only for a moment.

As he cradled Gracie in his arms, Dallas knew he loved her.

I love Gracie Henderson.

He couldn't say it. Not yet. It was too soon.

"I'll be here, Gracie. For as long as Misty needs me. I promise."

It didn't come out the way he wanted. Gracie eased back from him, until she stood two feet away. Her face looked sad.

"There can't be any more for us, Dallas."

"Why?" How deeply those words cut.

"It's too soon. You're still a novelty to Misty. You didn't even remember your own name."

"That doesn't mean—"

Gracie shook her head. "I know what it's like to be left alone, to feel like nobody loves you." Shadows crept into her eyes. "I won't let Misty feel that. She comes before us. She has to."

"I know."

But he ached to tell Gracie he loved her, ached to bring the light back into her eyes. Still, Dallas knew she would think he was just trying to salve her ego.

And he wasn't certain she'd ever believe him, if he didn't get his memory back.

He wanted—needed—Gracie's love.

Please heal me, he prayed.

The meeting took place six days later in Elizabeth Wisdom's office.

Gracie shuffled from one foot to the other to combat her growing apprehension. She couldn't look away from Dallas's expectant gaze.

"What is it, Sheriff?" Gracie asked.

"I received word that Mr. and Mrs. Henderson, Sr., have been located. They have been living in Australia for the past few months. I've been informed they will return stateside as soon as they are able to make arrangements."

Gracie swallowed, searching for moisture for her parched mouth. Would tomorrow be the only Father's Day Gracie would celebrate with both parents? she wondered.

"Thank you for all your help," Elizabeth was saying. She ushered the sheriff out, as if she sensed Dallas and Gracie needed a moment to absorb the information.

"My parents are coming." Dallas looked stunned.

A throb of fear tried to surface, but Gracie heard her Bible study leader's voice: *"Faith is an action, something you choose to do."*

God, are You there? Can I trust You?

"You must be excited," she said tentatively.

"I don't know how I feel. I never imagined… I don't even know what they look like."

"I'm sorry, I don't have a picture."

He'd already pored over the ones she did have, pried details from her that Gracie had shared with no one else—sad little bits of her history with her father, how alone she felt, unloved. The one thing she hadn't shared was his parents' rejection of her and Misty. Dallas was so open and loving. She couldn't hurt him by revealing their past actions. What good would it do? She had to focus on the future.

Recently she'd been letting hope take root inside. Dallas was so attentive, kind, understanding. It had been like dating all over again, only this time they hadn't had to do it through letters and phone calls. This time he was there to lend a hand, encourage her, share Misty. This time it was much more fulfilling. Gracie had seen what their little family could be.

She would fight for Dallas and Misty no matter what the cost to her.

"Well, I guess I'll get to know them when they get here. In the meantime, I want to ask you something. Promise you'll hear me out before you answer."

"What is it?"

"I want to teach Misty to ride."

"Absolutely not."

"Because you had a bad experience?"

"Because it's dangerous. Because she could get hurt. Because there are a hundred other things she could learn to do." Frustration ate through Gracie's control. She yanked open the door and stepped outside, stomped back to her own office, aware of Dallas following. "We talked about this before. You know how I feel," she cried once they were inside, out of other people's earshot.

"You're afraid she'll get hurt like you did. I know. Listen to me, will you?"

Gracie flopped down in her chair, frustrated by his request. Every single time she thought they were getting somewhere, Dallas pushed her too far. But this time she would not budge.

"It's not me who wants her to ride," he said. "Well, I do, but I haven't said anything to her yet."

"Then?"

"It's Rory. His mother thinks he's made so much progress that she's allowing him to go on the ranch's upcoming trail ride. Misty found out and now she wants to go, too. But she's afraid to ask you."

"Misty's not afraid to ask me anything."

"She is this time, Gracie." His dark eyes rested on her with a measure of sadness. "She told Rory you're afraid she can't do it."

"That isn't true. I'm concerned she'll be injured. I would die if that happened."

"Why do you automatically assume the worst scenario, Gracie?"

The question surprised her, but she shot back an answer. "Because it usually does."

"Usually?" Dallas shook his head. "I lost my memory and went missing. You had our baby. But you managed, you handled things, and I finally came back."

"With amnesia," she amended. "And you forgot what happened with my dad."

"That was all six years ago. What other bad things have happened that keep you chained by fear?"

She didn't answer that question, but muttered, "Why am I always the one who has to change? What about you?"

"How do you want me to change?" he asked reasonably.

"You could stop pushing me all the time. My decisions are based on what's best for Misty."

"Are they? How does keeping our daughter out of an activity the other children love help her?"

"Don't ask me anymore, Dallas," Gracie said softly. "I can't do it."

"And when Misty asks you?"

She didn't get a chance to answer, because Dallas slapped on his Stetson and left. A little while later she heard him talking to someone, and peeked out the window. Lady strutted around the paddock, head tossed back, mane flying as she ran free.

Dallas held no rope. He made no effort to constrain the beautiful animal. Instead he encouraged her, and when Lady finally moved closer, he touched her gently, all the while whispering assurances.

Gracie kept watching, becoming aware that Dallas didn't need to use words anymore. His actions, his demeanor—they'd convinced the horse that he could be trusted. Lady allowed him to slip on a bridle, danced for a moment, then nudged him with her head while he fastened the girth.

Soon Dallas was seated on Lady and she was walking around the paddock, obeying the touch of his hands on her flanks.

"I'm trying to trust you," Gracie murmured. "But…"

But. That was the whole problem in one word.

And for the life of her Gracie couldn't get past it.

"I'm not going to sing in the choir tomorrow morning, Mommy."

"Are you sick?" Gracie touched the smooth forehead, felt a cheek. "You don't feel hot. Is your tummy upset?"

"No."

Dallas watched mother and daughter soundlessly. He'd been afraid of this. He walked over to his daughter, knelt in front of her.

"What's wrong, Miss?"

"I can't sing in the choir."

"Why not? You sing beautifully. Miss Craft said you know all the words."

"That's not why." Misty stamped her toe on the floor.

"So what's the problem?"

"We have to go up steps. What if I miss one and fall down?"

"Then you get up."

"Everybody will laugh at me."

Gracie shot him a questioning look. "Have the other kids at church been laughing at you, Misty?" she asked.

"Nobody teased me."

Dallas lifted her in his arms, carried her to the love

seat and sat down with her on his knee. "Why don't you tell me what's wrong, Miss?" he coaxed gently.

"I'm scared." She tucked her head against his neck, nuzzled closer.

"Of falling off the step?"

"Sort of."

"What else?" He watched Gracie sink down opposite them, listening intently.

"It's s'posed to be a surprise," Misty whispered.

"I think it's okay if you tell me this one time." He covered her little hand with his, marveling at the daintiness of Misty's hand.

"I'm s'posed to sing a solo. You know, for Father's Day. Rory says that when I start, my voice gets all creaky and I sound like a stuck pig. I don't even know what a stuck pig sounds like."

"Neither does Rory." Dallas battled an urge to box little Rory's ears next time he saw him.

"Well, I don't think it's a nice sound. I don't want to squeal."

"I think you'll sound like a beautiful bird. I would be a very proud father to hear you sing in church tomorrow."

Misty wasn't convinced. "What if I forget that really high note?"

"What if you do? What's the most terrible thing that can happen?" He tickled her under the chin. "Will sharks eat you when you get in the pool? Will robbers come and take your piggy bank? What are you scared of?"

"People will laugh at me," Misty whispered. "Sometimes they do, you know. Mommy doesn't like it. She always makes us hurry away."

Dallas heard Gracie catch her breath, saw her blink back tears. But he couldn't comfort her now. Misty needed him to be strong.

"What else?"

"Mommy always tells me to be careful, and I try to be, but…"

"What, Miss?"

"I get afraid sometimes, Daddy."

Daddy. The word punched him in the stomach, sucked all his breath away.

Oh, what a Father's Day gift. *Thank You, Father of all.*

"Listen to me, my most darling Misty. We all get afraid sometimes."

"Not you."

"Are you kidding me? I'm afraid lots."

"Really?"

He couldn't make this up. Misty was too smart for that. So he spoke from his heart. "I'm afraid when I wake up every morning."

"You are? Why?" she asked, obviously shocked by his admission.

"I'm afraid because you might be gone away, and I won't get to tell you I love you, and that I'm very glad I'm your daddy."

"I'm not going anywhere," Misty assured him. "I like the ranch. What else?"

"Sometimes I get afraid I won't ever remember my past."

"Why does that make you scared?"

"You can remember stuff about when you were little, can't you, Miss?"

"Sure." She fiddled with his shirt button.

"I can't. I can't remember my mom kissing me good-night or my dad showing me how to ride a bike, or where I lived or if I had any sisters and brothers. I can't remember any of that, and it makes me feel like I'm all alone. That's when I get scared."

"So what do you do?"

"I pray. I ask God to help me. Then I get up and get going. God doesn't want me to be afraid, He wants me to ask Him to help me, and He wants me to keep being Dallas."

"Being Daddy," she corrected absently. "Do you think if I prayed God would help me?"

"I'm sure of it." Dallas clasped her hands in his, bowed his head and prayed out loud for his little girl to put her faith in God. "Does that help?"

"Yes. But I still don't think that I'll sing."

"You're the only one who can decide. If it scares you too much, then don't." Was it wrong to challenge a child?

Misty frowned. "Will you read me a story, Daddy?"

"Sure." He didn't care that he wasn't proficient at braille. Dallas intended to read to his daughter, to tuck her in, kiss her good-night. It was the least a real daddy could do.

When he came out of Misty's room an hour later, Gracie was in the pool, cleaving through the water with great purpose and strength. He debated going to her, but something inside told him to leave.

So he headed toward Lady's stall, led her into one of the rings.

And the entire time he worked with her he pleaded with God to help his wife and his daughter.

"And me," he begged as the moon rose high and

round. "Please, please, heal me. I love them. I need them. Isn't that why You brought me here?"

But though he waited long past midnight, no memory returned.

Chapter Nine

Gracie was up before the sun on Sunday morning.

She'd never gone to bed.

Tortured by Misty's lack of confidence, she wondered how much she'd damaged her child's self-assurance.

She thought of Dallas and how willing he'd been to reveal his own weakness in order to help Misty understand that everyone struggled to remain confident. How easily he'd taught her to turn to God for love and support.

Something Gracie should have done long ago.

Dallas's love was selfless. It freed Misty to grow and learn and become the child God wanted her to be. Dallas strengthened Misty with his love, while Gracie's imprisoned her child and made her feel helpless.

Gracie had spent the night praying to make the right decision. Now, as the sun's golden rays flooded her small patio, flickered across the onion skin pages of her Bible, she knew what she had to do. Dallas had shown her.

To make this family strong Gracie had to step back and allow Misty the opportunity to experience everything the ranch offered.

Everything.

"Mommy?" Misty stood at the door, tousled, her nightgown rumpled.

"Hi, sweetie." Gracie waited, relishing the moment when her daughter climbed into her lap and snuggled against her. "Did you have a good sleep?"

"Yes." Misty's fingers curled into her shirt.

"I'll have to go shower and change soon. Get ready for church. But I thought I'd sit here and watch the sun rise first. Do you want to watch, too?"

It was a secret code between them, which meant Gracie would describe the event in terms Misty could understand.

"Okay." The child lay still, listening carefully.

"Now the sun's like a big ball climbing up, up. It's almost over the hill. It's got a thousand arms all around it, reaching out. Can you feel the heat in its arms?"

"Yes." Misty tipped her chin up as the brilliant rays splashed her face. "I can feel it."

"That's your first sunrise, young lady."

"Oh." Misty considered that. "There are lots of firsts, aren't there, Mommy."

"Many many more for you, my sweet." She kissed her head.

"Some might be bad firsts."

"They might. But you're a Henderson, Misty. Henderson women are strong. We can stand a few bad times. It makes us stronger."

"I'm not a woman." Misty giggled. "I'm just a girl."

"A very smart, brave girl who is learning each day to do new things. I'm proud of you, honey."

"I didn't do nothing special. Not like Rory. He's learning to ride the horses."

"Is riding something you'd like to do, Misty?" Gracie asked quietly.

Her daughter tipped her head to one side. "I don't know. Horses are big."

"Some are. But most are very gentle creatures if you understand how to treat them. They know exactly how to step so they don't pinch my toes when I check them, for example."

"Daddy said horses understand human people so much they know how to help them sometimes."

"Yes." Hearing Misty call Dallas "Daddy" was so bittersweet that Gracie's heart squeezed each time she heard her say it. Daddy. Mommy. Family.

Misty remained silent for a long time. When she finally spoke, her voice was soft, hesitant. "Do you think I could learn to ride a horse, Mommy?"

"Of course you could learn." Gracie forced away the fear by sending a prayer Heavenward. "If you really wanted to."

"Enough to go on the trail ride?"

"Hmm. That's a big one. I don't know. What do you think?"

"Rory said it takes two whole hours and you don't get off the horse once. That's a long time."

"It is if you don't practice." Gracie squeezed her eyes closed. "I think it's like singing, Misty. The more you do it, the better you get."

"I heard you tell Daddy you fell off a horse when you were a little girl." Misty's voice shrank with each word. "You said you didn't ride after that. You sounded scared."

"Did I? Well, I was only three then. You're five." Gracie caught her breath. "Do you think I should learn to ride, Misty?"

"I don't know. Do you think I should sing in the choir today?" Her face was scrunched in confusion. "Maybe I'll mess it all up."

Gracie smoothed the bright curls, prayed for the right words. "Yes, maybe you will."

Misty frowned, as if she hadn't expected that.

"How would you feel if that happened, sweetie?"

"Dumb. But Daddy wouldn't care. And he's the one I'll be singing to. Because daddies like it when their kids do stuff. That's what Miss Craft said."

"Miss Craft is absolutely right."

"Now I don't know what to do," Misty complained.

"It is hard to decide, isn't it? I mean, if you make a mistake with the song and the kids laugh, that wouldn't be fun. But Dal—Daddy wouldn't care about a mistake. So I guess you have to decide which would be worse, not to sing to Daddy on Father's Day, and disappoint him, or sing and maybe make a mistake and risk the other kids laughing."

Misty frowned. "That's hard to decide."

"Yes. But think about this. Maybe if you decided to sing—I'm not saying you have to, but if you did— maybe it would help you know if you are strong enough to learn to ride."

"Like a test? Like swimming?" she asked. "First I had to try to float, and when I did that, I learned to kick my feet, and that helped me think I could move my arms, too. And then I was swimming. Like that?"

"Exactly like that, darling."

"'Cept I already know how to sing." Misty slid out of Gracie's lap, stood on the sun-warmed cement in her bare feet. "Do you think Daddy could show me the steps at church before it starts?"

"Well, you could ask him when he comes. Of course, you'd have to get dressed soon. We'd need to leave early."

"I'm always early," Misty informed her. "You're the one who's usually late because of your head-bed. Daddy says we can't let you go to church like that."

"Bed head," Gracie corrected automatically. "And he's *usually* teasing, though it might need a little help today. It smells like chlorine."

"Well, fix it, Mommy. I don't want to be late."

Her command issued, Misty hurried into the house and began hauling out her favorite cereal and milk. A moment later the refrain of her choir song floated out from the CD player, accompanied by Misty's sweet voice.

"Very well done, Mommy."

Dallas's low growl penetrated her thoughts. Gracie turned and saw him standing on the other side of the fence, dressed in his casual clothes, watching her. Approval glowed in his dark eyes, causing Gracie's pulse to flutter.

"That was a very big step."

"You heard."

"I didn't mean to. I was passing and almost called out, but I didn't want to disturb you. Are you all right?"

"I don't know," Gracie answered honestly, keeping her voice low as she rose and moved toward the fence. Lately the only private time she and Dallas had outside of work was the hour Misty was at choir practice, and she was beginning to realize it wasn't enough. She wanted more uninterrupted time with him to explore the relationship they were slowly rebuilding.

"I'm still scared for her."

"That's natural."

"I'm still not sure it was a good idea, but I'm trying to trust."

"That's the first step of faith, Gracie. And I know how you feel. I wake up with that same inner doubt every morning. And then I ask God to be with me."

"And that makes it better?"

"Not always." Dallas reached across the fence, tucked a strand of her hair behind her ear. "You didn't sleep?"

"No." She leaned into his touch, trying to remember if she'd ever felt like this when they'd been together. She didn't think so.

Love had been a novelty then, something she'd basked in, but usually felt too shy to display. Now she could hardly wait to touch Dallas, to feel his arm circling her waist or hugging her close. Uncertainty about how things would turn out couldn't stop her from relishing his nearness, reveling in the contact she craved.

She closed her eyes, savoring the moment as she covered his hand with hers.

"Oh, Gracie."

She almost didn't hear the broken whisper. He lifted her palm to his mouth and pressed a kiss in the center before curling her fingers around it.

"Why did you do that?"

"Because sometimes I need to touch you."

His stark answer blazed a path straight to her heart. She needed him, too. Needed to lean on his strength for a while, let him take control. Needed to share things with him, laugh with him, cry with him. She needed Dallas to help build the family she longed for.

"Why are you up so early?" she asked, noting a change in his demeanor.

"Elizabeth woke me. She had a call from my parents. I went on her computer, saw them, thanks to her Web camera. We talked for a bit."

Gracie froze, her breath strangled by fear's tentacles.

"My mom had a bit of a medical setback on the way to Canberra. They're clearing that up before they travel here. Nothing serious, apparently, but it's going to take more time before we're reunited."

"I'm sorry."

It was an automatic response, tinged by relief that for a little longer Misty and Dallas would be hers alone.

"It's okay." Disappointment sagged his broad shoulders. "I didn't recognize them, you know." The light in his eyes vanished. "I'm not sure why I thought I would."

She ached to gather him close, ease his hurt. But the fence and fear separated them.

"Maybe when you see them in person things will be different."

"Yeah. Maybe." He shook off the gloom, leaned over the fence and brushed her lips with his. "I'd better get going. See you in a bit, Gracie, love."

"Yes. See you."

As she watched him walk away, the verse Gracie had read over and over through the predawn hours returned with startling clarity.

"I am leaving you with a gift—peace of mind and heart. And the peace I give isn't fragile like the peace the world gives. So don't be troubled or afraid."

"I will not be afraid," she whispered. "Help me not be afraid."

"Mommy! Aren't you coming?"

"Yes, darling. I'm on my way."

Gracie retrieved her Bible and her coffee cup and walked into the house with new purpose. She couldn't handle the fear on her own.

But she didn't have to.

God would help. All she had to do was trust Him.

He thought his chest would burst with pride.

Misty's pure, clear voice carried around the church like a bell as she sang about a father's love.

They'd talked about how to combat her nervousness. "You sing right to me, Miss. Forget everybody else. Okay?"

"Yes, Daddy."

Gracie's slim hand slid into his and squeezed tightly as Misty soared through her final notes. The congregation sighed. Then the choir chimed in and the cantata proceeded. There were four soloists in all, but their daughter was the best. And when the service was finally dismissed, Dallas couldn't help basking in the congratulations everyone offered.

"I'm her father," he told an old woman who was chatting with Misty.

"You're a very fortunate man, then."

"Yes, I am." He lifted Misty into his arms and hugged her so tightly she protested. "You were great, Miss."

"Did you like your song, Daddy?"

"I loved it. I wish I'd thought to borrow a video camera and record it."

"Miss Craft had someone record the cantata. We can buy a copy from her." Gracie brushed a smudge of dust from Misty's face. "It was really lovely, honey."

She wiggled, wanting to be put down. Dallas let her go, winced at the emptiness of his arms.

"It was a good test, Mommy," the little girl said, her smile wide. "Now I know what I want to do."

"What's that?"

"I want to learn how to ride a horse. I want to go on the trail ride."

Dallas watched the color leach from Gracie's beautiful face. But she smiled as she said, "That's good, sweetie."

He slid an arm around her waist, squeezed to show his support.

"I'm starving," he said. "How about if I take my girls to lunch? A celebration for Misty's new singing career."

"No!" Misty glanced at her mother for guidance.

"I think we should go back to our place," Gracie murmured.

"Okay." Dallas sensed some secret message passing between the two. "Let's go."

As Gracie drove them back to the ranch, he watched her. She answered Misty's never-ending questions absently, her attention obviously elsewhere.

"I think it's time I saw somebody about getting my license back," he said as he held out a hand to help Gracie from the truck. Misty had already scurried inside. "Thanks to the sheriff and Elizabeth and all the paperwork we filled out I've got my identity back, but apparently I have to retake the driving test."

"Do you remember driving?" Gracie asked as they walked toward the open front door.

"No." But suddenly he did. A sports car, with the top down. Gracie was laughing beside him, her hair streaming in the wind as she held up one hand. A gold circlet glittered on her ring finger.

"Dallas?"

"Yeah?" He shook his head. She was holding the door, waiting for him. "Did I used to own a red sports car?"

"You rented one once."

Gracie moved to the kitchen. Her tone didn't invite more questions, but he couldn't let it go. "Was it around the time we were married?"

She paused, twisted to look at him. "Yes."

"I had this flash of it. We were riding in the car. You were holding your hand up. You wore a gold band." He stared at her bare finger.

"My wedding ring," she said, so quietly he had to lean close to hear. "I took it off a couple of years ago. I didn't think you were coming back."

Shouldn't she have come looking for him once more, before she gave up?

"Surprise! Happy Father's Day, Daddy."

Only then did Dallas realize that Misty, with Gracie's help, had made special plans to celebrate his day. If his heart had been full before it almost burst now as she pulled open the patio door, indicating the table outside, fully set.

"It looks beautiful." He mouthed a thank-you to Gracie over Misty's head as he hugged his child. "Did you do all this?"

"Mommy helped." She pulled out a chair. "You have

to sit here. It's the father's place. What do I do now, Mommy?"

"I think we should cook the hamburgers. Maybe Dallas could do that while I bring out the other food."

"Sure." He stepped onto the deck, lit the grill.

Gracie returned inside. Misty hopped across the bricks toward him.

"I'm glad you're my daddy," she said. "Rory doesn't got a daddy."

"That's too bad."

"Yeah." Misty shrugged. "I gave him a hug. I know what it feels like not to have a daddy. It's lonely."

Dallas gathered her close, sank down on one of the chairs while they waited for the grill to heat.

"I'm sorry I couldn't be here for all of the other Father's Days, Misty. I wanted to be but I just couldn't remember."

"I know. It's okay." She fiddled with his tie. "When do you think I'll take my first riding lesson?"

From the corner of his eye, Dallas saw Gracie in the doorway, carrying a tray. She stopped suddenly, rattling some of the things on it.

"I don't know. Maybe after lunch we could go ask Emily about it."

"Can't you teach me to ride a horse?"

"I don't know if I've ever taught anyone to ride. We'll ask Mommy after lunch. Okay?"

"Okay." She wiggled out of his lap and scurried off toward the fence, humming the song she'd sung earlier.

"Is everything all right?" Dallas lifted the tray from Gracie's hands, set it on the table.

"Yes, thanks." She forced a smile but it didn't reach her eyes.

Something was wrong.

There was no time to discuss whatever it was during lunch, and after they'd cleaned up, Misty insisted on visiting Emily, who advised them that Misty could join the class the very next day.

Emily pulled Dallas aside after their chat. "You could help her by getting her used to the animals. The kids learn much quicker if they've had some exposure to the horses and aren't afraid."

As they started back to the house, Misty hung on to her parents' hands, swinging between them. "I'm going to be behind the other kids," she mumbled. "They've been taking riding lessons for a long time."

"Why don't we stop and check on Lady?" Dallas watched Gracie, but she kept her mask of control firmly in place.

"Can we, Mommy?"

"I guess."

At the paddock where the horse was corralled, Dallas stuck his thumb and finger in his mouth and whistled. The mare trotted over, ears perked.

"Hello, pretty Lady," he murmured, brushing his hand over her nose. "If you speak to them carefully and gently, horses aren't afraid, Miss."

"I know Patch was afraid when I was feeding him grass, but I didn't think Lady would be afraid. Lady sounds lots bigger, Daddy." Misty chewed on her bottom lip as if she were working a puzzle in her mind. "Are you sure Lady was afraid?"

"Pretty sure, honey. That's why I didn't want you two

to meet until I made sure Lady knew we wanted to be friends. Sometimes people are mean to them, and horses have very good memories. They're very careful about who they trust. Here, you can pet her neck." He guided her hand there.

"Hello, horsey. My daddy says your name is Lady. Mine's Misty. Oh!" She giggled as the horse nuzzled her hand. "Why's she doing that, Daddy?"

"She's looking for a treat. Lady likes carrots as much as you liked those fudge brownies your mom made. But Lady's not allowed to have chocolate," he cautioned. "It would make her very sick. Horse tummies can't have brownies."

"I want to feed her a carrot."

"Keep your voice down, Miss. Horses like it better if you don't make sudden moves or loud noises around them. Lady has to learn to trust you, just like you have to learn to trust her."

The way your mom has to learn to trust me.

"Can I please have a carrot, Daddy?" Misty whispered in exaggerated tones.

"I'll go get one. You stay with Dal—Daddy." Gracie offered him a quick smile, then hurried toward her office, where she kept a small bag of carrots in the medicine fridge.

His heart did a two-step when she turned at the door, stared at him with those sky-blue eyes.

Please let us be a family soon. Please let her love me as much as I love her.

Chapter Ten

Gracie felt like a schoolgirl on her first date.

Nervous. Giddy. Hopeful.

Scared.

Which was utterly ridiculous.

She was married to the man!

But Dallas had asked Gracie to have dinner with him tonight, after Rory had shown up to invite Misty to eat at his place. And since this would be Gracie's first date with Dallas in six years, she was on tenterhooks, wondering what he expected from it.

"Dinner is served, madam."

Her husband bowed at the waist like the butler at Elizabeth's ancestral ranch home. Gracie had visited her there, on the other side of Dallas, several times, and left intimidated by the grandeur of the place. Thankfully, the Bar None was nothing like that. Her little house certainly wasn't, despite Dallas's acting.

Gracie sat on the chair he held out for her, let him spread her napkin in her lap.

"It's Father's Day. I should be cooking dinner for you."

"I'll take you up on that next year." His gaze promised her a future.

Dallas cleared his throat, continued. "On the menu tonight we have shrimp cocktail, a garden salad with raspberry dressing, roast chicken, whipped potatoes, French-style green beans and a savory gravy. The dessert is my surprise."

"Sounds lovely." She waited until he returned with the shrimp and sat down. "I had no idea you could cook like this."

"I'm not sure I can. But the mess hall cook owed me a favor and I decided it was time for payback." He grinned, winked. "Go ahead. Try it."

He'd dressed the patio table with one of her good cloths, chosen glassware over Misty's usual plastic, and selected Gracie's mom's two remaining china dinner plates. In the center of the table he'd placed a bowl of wild roses he'd picked on the way back from the visit with Lady, a visit Rory had interrupted.

"It looks really lovely, Dallas. Thank you."

He reached for her hand. "Shall I say grace?"

She nodded, unable to speak.

"Lord, we thank You for this beautiful day, for Your love and for Misty. Help her to have a good time with Rory and help us enjoy these gifts You've given us. In Jesus's name." Dallas kissed Gracie's fingertips, then let her hand go.

In the background the soft sounds of her favorite guitar music broke the silence.

"It seems I know this song." Dallas tilted his head, hummed a few bars.

"You should. She's your favorite guitarist. The CD is one you bought."

"Oh." He listened a moment longer, then picked up his fork. *"Bon appetit."*

"Do you think Misty's okay? She hasn't spent much time in new places—"

"Misty's fine, Gracie."

She wondered if Dallas was impatient with her. He didn't look angry.

"That sun still has a lot of heat," he stated. "I'm glad we've got a bit of shade here. And it's the perfect spot to watch the sunset."

"The sunsets here are spectacular," she agreed. "The summer evenings aren't nearly as long as they were at home, though. It used to stay light till almost ten o'clock on the longest day."

"Do you miss North Dakota?"

"Sometimes. I had some good friends there who helped me through the rough parts."

"And your father?"

Why was he asking questions about the past?

"He was a hard man. We didn't always agree. Maybe we were too much alike."

"Did you love him?"

Gracie froze, her fork dropping against her plate with a loud ping. "I tried," she whispered finally, pushing away the tears. "He didn't seem to want it."

"I pity him, then. I think that love is a precious commodity and you should take every morsel that's offered. Finished with that?"

"Yes. Thanks. It was delicious." She watched him carry their dishes to the kitchen, return with salad.

"I added a couple of things myself. Can you guess what?"

"Dill. Parsley? And lots of onion."

"How did you know?"

"The cook never uses onion in the salad because so many kids won't eat it." Gracie lifted an eyebrow. "And besides, you always used to love onion in your salad."

Dallas grinned. "Still do. Did we eat out much?"

Just when she got comfortable, he shot out these questions about the past.

"In Dallas, yes. Turtleford was a little town. There weren't many places to go. Besides, I usually cooked for my dad when I was home."

"Did you like school?"

"Yes."

"But all that ended when Misty came along."

"Yes, but I went back to school, finished my classes and got my degree, though it took me longer. Besides, I don't begrudge anything for Misty." Worry nudged its way in again. "I hope she's doing all right. Sometimes she doesn't—"

"She needs other people in her life, Gracie. And we need time together, too. If a problem arises, we'll deal with it. Okay?"

Shame rushed through her. He was trying so hard to build their relationship, and he had no memories, nothing to go on. Didn't he ever worry?

"Sorry." She lifted her glass. "To your great cooking."

He clinked his against it, chuckled. "Yeah. I chop a mean dill stalk, lady."

A comfortable silence lingered between them for a

while. Gracie eventually broke it with small talk, with sharing. It was easier than she'd thought.

"I wonder if I should think about voice lessons for Misty. Until I heard that solo this morning, I never realized how good she is."

"Elizabeth might know someone." Dallas carried in their salad plates, returned with the main course, then sat down once more. He lifted his fork, touched the potatoes, but paused. "What happened to you this morning in church, Gracie?"

"I don't know what you mean."

"After the service. Misty talked about the trail ride and you froze like an icicle. I thought you were ready to let her try riding."

"I am." Gracie gulped, sipped some water to moisten her parched throat. "But…"

"Tell me. I'll help if I can," he promised, leaning across the table to stroke his fingers over her forearm.

"The trail ride," she blurted.

"If you're that much against it—"

"I'm not exactly thrilled, but I recognize that I can't stand in her way anymore, as you so adequately pointed out." Gracie glanced down, watched his fingers thread through hers. She lifted her lids, met his compassionate gaze. "I won't be the reason she's afraid. I'm trying to trust God."

His fingers pressed hers. "Good for you."

"But…I can't go with her."

"Sure you can. Other parents will be going along." He paused, made a face. "Oh, you mean because you can't ride."

"I would learn to ride if it meant I could go with her.

But the certification board will be here that day, Dallas. As the resident vet I have to be around to answer any questions, show my qualifications and whatever else they want. It's a stipulation the state makes as part of the process to grant Elizabeth's permanent license for this place. There's no way I can ask for the day off to go on a trail ride."

"Maybe they could change the day of the ride."

She shook her head. "Not without disrupting the ranch's schedule." Cold feathered up her back, and she shivered. Gracie drew her hand from his, tasted the potatoes absently.

"There has to be a way." Dallas stabbed his meat as if attacking the problem. "Misty will probably change her mind ten times before then, anyway. We'll figure it out."

"Of course we will."

Ashamed by the pall she'd cast over his lovely meal, Gracie struggled to re-create the mood, summoning every bit of gaiety she could gather as she teased him and laughed at his silly jokes.

"I haven't eaten this late for years. I didn't realize how hungry I was. It was great, Dallas. Thank you."

"We haven't finished yet. There's still dessert waiting."

"Later, maybe? I'm too full right now."

"What about coffee?"

"Sure."

He refused to let her help clear the table. A short while later he carried out two cups, hers perfectly creamed.

"You make a mean cup of coffee," she teased after tasting it.

He saluted. "I aim to please, ma'am."

"Always the cowboy." She chuckled. "I haven't seen you in sneakers since you got those boots."

"Sneakers?" He grinned and thrust his booted feet out in front of him. "I'm a good ol' Texas boy."

"I know. I used to wonder how you got on with big-city folks. Your rapport with the animals was so amazing. You seemed happiest with them."

"Well, I probably dazzled the big boys with my charm and wit." He shifted his chair closer, pointing out a few species of birds that fluttered in the treetops.

"Your memory in that area doesn't seem to be damaged," she mused. "I wish we could figure out what happened to the rest."

"Does it matter?" He looked at her, his eyes unfathomable. "Aren't I the same person whether I remember the past or not?"

"Do you feel the same?" Even as she asked the question, Gracie wondered what it would lead to. It was almost as if he was testing her.

"I feel like I could stay here for a long time. Not because I'm hiding but because I can help. Maybe it's not the same work I did before, but I think I'm giving back to the ranch."

"Of course you are. That little autistic girl had never even acknowledged her mother until you let her feed that fawn. You and the animals have done that for her."

"Thanks."

"I mean it. I don't know what your plans are, but I'm sure Elizabeth would be thrilled if you decided to stay here permanently."

"She's got me listed on the payroll as a trainer now."

He laughed. "I have no idea what I'm training anyone to do, but it's nice to know someone thinks I'm worth paying more. And speaking of that, I want to help out with expenses."

"What expenses?"

"Misty's. Yours. I can chip in, Gracie. It doesn't cost much to stay here and there's no place to spend money, anyway." He reached in his pocket, handed her a check. "Here."

She hadn't realized it, but of course Elizabeth would have made sure he had his own account to deposit his payroll checks into. Gracie kept thinking of Dallas as needy, and he wasn't. Not anymore. He was earning decent money, judging by the size of the check. He'd made friends on the ranch, lots of them. Next week he was supposed to go for his driver's license.

Her heart squeezed.

"I don't want this, Dallas." She handed it back. "We're fine. We don't need anything."

He looked as if she'd hit him. "But I want to help. It's my job to take care of my family." When she didn't say anything, his jaw twitched, then hardened. "Put it in the bank then, I don't care. But I refuse to take it back, Gracie. It's the least I can do after six years."

Dallas was trying to make up for the past, and she'd hurt him.

He'd done everything he could to repair the damage his absence had caused, and she'd shoved this latest offer back in his face. Was that what a wife did to her husband?

Shamed, Gracie fingered the check. "I started an account for Misty's education," she whispered. "We could add it to that, if you want. If we get enough she'll be able to attend the college of her choice."

"Fine."

Feeling bad wasn't enough. She had to apologize, bring that light back into Dallas's eyes. "I'm sorry."

He gazed at the sky for a long time before facing her. "It doesn't matter."

"Yes, it does." She had to make him understand. "It's not that I don't appreciate what you do for us, Dallas. You've made Misty so happy. She adores you and she's much more confident with you around."

"And you?" His perceptive eyes pierced through her. "What do you appreciate me for?"

"Your honesty," Gracie whispered. "The way you won't let me back down from anything. The way you're always there to cheer me on. The way you pointed me back to God."

Her answers, though they came from her heart, didn't seem to satisfy him.

"Is that all?"

"That is a great deal, Dallas. You haven't been back that long, but you've impacted everyone on this ranch."

"I'm not trying to impress anyone. I only care about what you think."

"I think you're a decent, honorable man who's trying his hardest to get his life in order after a very trying time," she murmured. "I think we're blessed to have you back."

He studied her for so long Gracie grew uncomfortable. "What's really on your mind, Dallas?"

"The future. How I fit into it." He picked up her hand, ran his fingers over the place where her wedding band should have been. "What's in our future, Gracie?"

"I can't answer that."

The uncertainty in his eyes hurt to watch, so she studied the horizon.

Dallas cupped her cheek, turned her to face him. "Do you see me as your husband? Us as a family?" he asked, his voice lacking the firm conviction she'd always heard before.

"I want to." She brushed away a mosquito. "I hope so."

"But you're afraid to look that far ahead, is that it?"

"You've dealt with a lot, Dallas. Finding out who you are, figuring out what you want to do, meeting Misty, me. It's a lot to get through in such a short time. Soon your parents will be here and you'll want to spend time with them, get to know them, talk about your past."

And I'll be left out.

"Are you sorry you married me, Gracie?"

"No," she gasped, stunned. "Marrying you was the best thing I ever did."

"But you wouldn't do it again." His mouth twisted in a wry grimace. "I see."

"I never said that."

"Then what are you saying?" he demanded. "Explain it to me. Bluntly."

"I'm saying that we got married very quickly. We weren't married that long before…before whatever happened to you took you away. We've been apart a long time."

"And you've changed."

"We both have changed, Dallas. But you're here, I'm here. We have this place and this space in time to make sure that our next step will be the right one."

"Implying our marriage wasn't."

"Stop putting words in my mouth." She got up, walked to the pool fence.

"I'm sorry." His breath warmed her ear as his arms went around her waist. "I'm pushing you too hard, I know that."

"Then don't do it. Enjoy what we have here and now."

"I can't." His lips brushed her neck. "I feel like nothing in my world is nailed down, and I need it to be. I need to know that you won't take off or tell me to leave if I mess up or make a mistake or step on your toes. I need...something."

"You have quite a lot." She turned in his arms, faced him. "You have a daughter who thinks you walk on water. You have a wife who quite enjoys it when you hold her like this." She smiled at him, pressed her lips to his cheek.

"Oh." His eyes began to glow. He kissed her tenderly, his hands holding her head.

"I'm not running away or telling you to leave," she whispered, stroking his jaw. "But I can't give you any guarantees, Dallas. I'm still finding my own way. But there is someone who understands what you're going through. You can always talk to Him."

"I know." Dallas kissed the top of her head, turned her so they could both watch the sun sink into the west. "I hope He understands how hard it is for me to let go of you."

With Misty bursting through the door just then, Gracie wondered if she'd actually heard his words.

After he'd tucked in their daughter, read her a story and kissed her good-night, Dallas returned to the patio to sit beside Gracie, watching the big moon fill the dark sky. When the time came, he kissed her good-night so sweetly her heart ached.

It was then she knew their present situation couldn't go on much longer.

If only his parents would delay their return. If only she could make him love her so much he'd never allow them to even consider taking Misty away from her.

If only.

"That was great, Misty. You're doing very well. Can you get off by yourself?"

"Sure." After two weeks of lessons and practice, she almost made it, needing Emily's help only for the very first step onto the structure all the children used when dismounting from their horses. "Did you see me, Mommy? Did you see me?"

"I did. It was a great ride, honey." Gracie inhaled several deep, cleansing breaths. No fear. God was in charge.

Would it ever get easier?

"How did you know to bend over Patch's neck like that?"

"Daddy told me yesterday. He said Patch likes it best when we whisper things to him. So I did. I whispered that I thought he's now the best horse on the whole ranch. He really liked that." She patted her mount's neck, held out a carrot.

The horse rubbed his head against her arm, then daintily plucked the carrot from Misty's grasp. She giggled, stepped down the stairs. Once on the ground she reached for Gracie's hand.

"Daddy tells me lots of things that horses like. He says I have to think like a horse and then I'll *know* what to do."

"Does he, darling?" Gracie glanced around, saw

Dallas in the neighboring paddock, struggling with a colt. He grinned at her, waved a hand, and she waved back. The young horse chose that moment to escape. Dallas looked so surprised she burst out laughing.

"I like it when you laugh, Mommy. It makes me think of fuzzy slippers and the pool splashing me."

"Hmm, that's quite a combination." As they strolled down the path toward home, Gracie couldn't help glancing over her shoulder. Dallas hadn't moved. He was still watching them. "What should we have for dinner?"

"Daddy likes that chicken you make."

"Yes, but once a week is enough. How about spaghetti and meatballs?"

"That's his favorite," Misty said so loudly the cook in the mess hall could have heard.

"I know." Gracie was talking to the air. Misty was hurrying ahead, confident, independent, happy. Exactly what Gracie wished for her daughter.

So why did she have the horrible feeling that any day now the ax would fall?

Misty set the table, then went to play with her dollies. Gracie put on a praise tape, hoping it would lift the feeling of dread that would not let up, no matter how hard she prayed.

When the meatballs were cooking in the oven, she and Misty went out to the pool for a cooling swim while they waited for Dallas to join them. They'd just climbed out of the water when he arrived, letting himself in through the gate.

"My two favorite bathing beauties," he teased, scooping Misty up for a hug and a kiss before he set her down again.

"Now it's Mommy's turn," she ordered, giggling.

"It certainly is. Hello, Mommy."

"Hi." She couldn't figure out what he was waiting for, but finally, exasperated, Gracie leaned forward and kissed him on the lips.

Immediately his arm slipped around her neck, and when she would have drawn away, he held her in place, deepening the kiss until her heart sang with joy.

"Now that's a welcome," he murmured.

"If you two ever get finished kissing, I want to go in the pool again before supper."

Dallas winked at Gracie. "Do we have time for one more kiss?"

"I think maybe one," she agreed, her heart bursting with love for him.

She'd dreamed of him last night, of them. They'd been at the arboretum. She'd been dressed in the beautiful white gown with the ballerina skirt he'd talked about that first day. He'd been wearing a white shirt, black trousers, his boots, of course, and holding his Stetson to shield them while he kissed her.

"This is forever, Gracie," he'd whispered.

"Isn't Mommy coming?"

She blinked in surprise. Dallas was no longer bending over her, but was now with Misty, in the pool.

So much for dreams.

"Yes, I'm coming. I challenge you to a race across the pool, Misty Henderson. And it starts now."

Maybe she couldn't have tomorrow, or next month or next year.

But she had today.

Chapter Eleven

"She's going to do well on the ride, Gracie. Misty has a knack for knowing how to move with the animal." Dallas fingered a sun-bleached curl caressing his wife's neck. "You can see how confident she is, how easily she rides after only a month. She's not afraid at all."

"Let's go once more around the corral to make sure."

"Once for her? Or once for you?" he asked, so quietly Misty couldn't possibly hear.

"Once for me. I had no idea riding a horse could be so…painful." Gracie wiggled in the saddle and he got the message, tried to hide his laughter.

"It isn't painful. Unless you insist on doing the accelerated Gracie course. Learn to ride in less than five hours."

"When I make up my mind, I like to get on with it."

"When I make up my mind, I don't change it. I'm marrying you, Dallas. So don't think I'll give you a chance to back out."

"Dallas?"

He blinked and the world righted itself. A short-haired, more mature version replaced the Gracie of his flashback.

"Dallas!"

"Yeah. I'm okay. Everything's fine." He pushed back the fog. "A little brain fade. Misty, the reins are too loose."

"I know. I'm fixing them."

"Good girl." He let Lady trail behind Gracie's horse to give himself time to regroup. So close. Why couldn't he remember all of it? "Relax, Gracie. You look like you're suffering."

"That's because I am," she snapped, sliding off her horse as soon as it arrived at the mounting block. "I don't know if I can even walk home."

"If you asked me nicely, I'd offer to carry you home."

She blushed a deep red at his whisper. "I think I'd better walk."

Dallas motioned to a wrangler he'd spoken with earlier, anticipating that his girls would want an early break.

"Usually you don't get to walk away after a ride," he reminded them quietly. "What do we do, Miss?"

"Put away the tack, brush down the horse, give it a drink and a treat."

"Right on. But since Mommy's, um…tired," he said, when Gracie shot him a glare, "Luke said he'd take care of our animals."

"Thank you, Luke," Misty chirped. "Patch, here's your carrot." She giggled as she always did when the horse gently bunted her back before stealing the carrot so fast her hand hung there empty for a second. "Thank you for the lovely ride, Patch. See you tomorrow."

"Yeah." Gracie rubbed her right hip. "Thanks a lot, horse."

"Her name is Minnie. She's the oldest horse on the whole ranch." Misty tucked her hand into Dallas's and trotted along beside him as they left the corral. "She's slow. I like Patch better."

"Personally, I like walking."

Gracie's brows lowered when Dallas snickered. He faked a cough.

"It's getting late, Miss. Remember your promise. Straight to bed with no fuss."

"I remember. I can hardly wait for the trail ride. It's going to be so much fun." She let go of his hand and skipped ahead, moving confidently as she tapped her fingertips against each of the posts.

"You're sure she's ready?" Gracie whispered, clutching his arm.

He threaded his fingers with hers. "She's ready."

"But what if—" She cut herself off, shook her head. "No, I refuse to go there."

"Good. I appreciate you trusting me with Misty's safety tomorrow, Gracie. It's such an honor. I know this isn't easy for you, and I promise I won't let anything happen."

"I know. I trust you."

Thank You, God.

For once Misty's bedtime ritual flew past. Dallas listened to her prayer, then tucked her in.

"Daddy?"

"Yes, Miss."

Misty leaned over, beckoned him near and whispered in his ear. "I'm kind of glad Mommy isn't coming tomorrow."

"Why is that?"

"I don't think she likes riding the horse. She kept sighing the whole time. She wouldn't have any fun at all. 'Specially not on old Minnie."

"Maybe you're right. G'night, Miss."

"Night, Daddy. See you tomorrow. Oh, I forgot to tell God thanks for the trail ride."

"You go ahead and thank Him. I want to talk to your mom."

"She's swimming. I can hear the water splashing." Misty grinned. "The window's open."

"I don't know how I could be your father," he said, tickling her chin. "You're too smart for me."

Dallas left the room as she began reciting all the things about the trail ride that she was thankful for. Outside, Gracie was plowing through the pool, as if trying to set an Olympic record. He put the kettle on, filled her small blue teapot with boiling water and a mint tea bag, then carried it outside, where he waited until she'd tired herself out.

"Thanks," she gasped, grasping the hand he held out and allowing him to pull her from the pool.

He wrapped her in the huge bath sheet she'd left on a chair, tucking in one corner like a sarong. He draped another towel across her shoulders in case she was chilled.

"Thank you."

"My pleasure." He waited until she was seated, then handed her a cup. "I made you some tea."

"Lovely." She savored the aroma with her eyes closed. "You spoil me, Dallas."

"It's my privilege." He sat down beside her, reached for her hand and brushed his lips across her knuckles. "One of many. Besides, you deserve to be spoiled."

"Too bad I didn't record that," she teased. But she didn't pull her hand away.

"Don't need to. I'm happy to repeat it whenever you want." And he would. Just to see her smile. "I'd like to do more," he murmured, wondering if Gracie truly understood how much he wanted everything that went with a real marriage.

"What would you like your life to look like in ten years, Gracie?"

"Ten years?" She gazed at him in surprise. "Misty will be fifteen then."

"Do you want more children? Or is Misty enough?"

"I…don't know." She didn't look at him. "I never thought about it."

"A ranch would be a wonderful place to raise kids," he murmured, studying the scene in front of them. Horses grazing in green pastures linked by white fences. The trails, the buildings, the barn, the dining hall. "I don't know where Elizabeth got the idea for this place, but it's fantastic. I haven't seen a single child who's come here fail to love the place."

"Once the licensing is done, Elizabeth has plans to see about starting a school here. She wants to integrate education into the Bar None philosophy."

A curious note in her voice snagged his attention. "Will you send Misty to school here?" he asked.

"We'd have to, at least at first. My contract is for six months, till November." Gracie frowned at him. "Do you think it wouldn't be good for her?"

She was asking his opinion. Was Gracie finally seeing them as a family?

"I don't think you can know that. I don't see why it wouldn't work out very well, but I guess only time will tell." He hesitated over the next words, but pushed them out because he needed to know. "What if I never remember anything, Gracie?"

She studied him, a funny smile on her lips. "To quote you, I don't think you can know that. Why?" She studied him more intently. "Do you think you won't?"

"I don't know. I got another flash when we were riding. It must have been from before we got married." He told her about it.

"That's good."

"Is it?" He wasn't sure. "It's like trying to put together a jigsaw puzzle without most of the pieces."

"Frustrating," she said.

"Very. I want my life back." *I want you back.* "But I don't know exactly what that entails. You don't like to talk about our past."

Silence yawned between them. For a few moments Dallas almost felt as if he could hear the sun sizzling into the glowering cloud on the western horizon as it set. Maybe he shouldn't have asked.

"What do you want to know?"

He shifted on the lounge so he could face her. "Everything."

So she told him, laid out the details of that first meeting and their subsequent communication via phone. She told him about his visits to the campus, their cheap and cheerful dates every time he managed a trip her way. She told him about his dream to someday have his own research team.

And finally she told him about the secret plans they'd made to be married, how they'd told her father, his reaction.

When she was finished, Dallas still wasn't satisfied. "You make it sound so happy," he murmured.

"It was, mostly."

Except for her father. He hadn't approved. Well, Dallas couldn't fault him there. Being a father himself offered a different perspective on having your daughter snatched away from you.

"But why did I leave? Why wasn't I with you? Why hadn't I made plans for our future? I can't understand that."

Gracie looked away. He remembered she'd had the same reaction once before.

"Did you have the impression that I didn't want to make a home for us, that I was going to continue the way I had been?" he asked, hating the idea, but desperate to know if he'd really been so thoughtless.

"You always loved traveling, Dallas," she said.

He grimaced at her carefully chosen words and the picture of him she was drawing.

"It would have been hard for you to give that up."

"But I married you. What did you expect would happen?"

"We never really discussed it. You understood that I had a couple more years of school. I thought you wanted me to finish. You'd keep on doing what you'd been doing, and when I was through, we'd talk about our next step then."

"And in the meantime I'd just keep wandering across the country, stopping by like a—a visitor?" He rubbed the space between his eyebrows, feeling anger bubbling inside him. "That's crazy. It's like long-distance dating. Irresponsible. Certainly not marriage!"

"It was the only one I had," she cried. Crystal droplets clung to the tips of her lashes. "Stop yelling at me, Dallas. It wasn't my fault."

Stupid, how stupid was he? "Of course it wasn't. *I* was the problem, Gracie. I'm sorry." He ran his palm down her arm, trying to erase the pain. "I can't understand what I was thinking."

"I can't explain that," she sniffed. "You never spoke about the future much. You just kept saying things would work out."

Serious doubts assailed Dallas. Was this the kind of man he'd been? Willing to leave his wife behind while he went off doing his thing, expecting her to sit there waiting for whenever he deigned to show up?

No wonder Gracie wasn't ready to discuss the future with him. She probably figured that the moment he was himself, he'd take off again. New respect filled him at what she'd endured.

"I don't know what the future holds, Gracie love." He rose, drew her upright so he could see into her eyes. "I don't know if I'll ever remember who I was, but I promise you one thing."

"You don't have to."

"Yes, I do. I promise you that no matter what happens, I'm here for the long term. If you want to move after your six months, fine. But until that time, I'll be here. I can't make up for the past, but I can promise you that I'll face whatever is in the future with you."

She didn't look convinced.

"You don't know what could happen," she whispered. "Something might come up that will change your mind. I don't want you to think you have to honor your promise."

"I'm not going anywhere, Gracie. I'm here until you tell me to go."

After searching his face for several moments, she finally nodded. "Okay. But if you change your mind—"

"Not going to happen. Didn't I promise for better or for worse?"

"Yes."

"I intend to honor that promise." He could no more have stopped himself from kissing her than he could stop breathing. Whatever he'd been, whatever he'd done, Gracie was his one constant, and he would not let go. In time she'd see that.

"You need to rest. Sweet dreams, my love." Dallas wanted to tell her how much he adored her, how he woke up yearning to hear her voice, how he fell asleep imagining the day she would welcome him into her life full-time.

But he wouldn't talk about love now.

Better to wait until the trail ride was over, until she saw how groundless her fears for Misty were. When she'd accepted that God was the best protector Misty could ever have, when she realized she could trust him to care for their daughter, then Dallas would propose again.

And this time he'd make sure she understood that he wanted to be a full-time husband in a full-time marriage. He could wait for that.

After all, now that he'd found her, they had all the time in the world.

Chapter Twelve

Gracie stood on the sidelines, nervously watching as Dallas checked Misty's horse and tack for what seemed the hundredth time.

Whenever I am afraid, I will trust in You, she thought, sending a prayer to Heaven.

"Have you got your juice snack, honey?" she asked, only now realizing how large Patch was, how high up her baby sat.

"Mommy, you asked me that already."

"Did I? Oh. Sorry."

"I have my juice, I have my jacket. I will be careful. I will obey Daddy. Okay?"

"I love you, Misty."

"I love you, too, Mommy. This is going to be so much fun."

"Try not to worry, Gracie. Remember, God is in control." Dallas brushed her cheek with his fist, his smile understanding. "It's only a few hours. We'll be back before you know it."

"Dallas," Gracie whispered, staring up at him. "Please—"

"I know." He bent his head and kissed her with a tenderness she'd never before felt so deeply. "Remember, she's my daughter, too."

"Yes."

He squeezed her shoulder one last time. Then, at a shout from the trail leader to mount up, he vaulted into his saddle and pulled on the Stetson he was seldom without. He studied her for a long moment, then bent down. Gracie stepped nearer.

"If you start to worry," he said, "pray. I'll be praying for you." After touching her hair, he gathered the reins, told Misty how to direct her horse, and they slowly meandered out of the corral.

Gracie watched until someone nudged her arm.

"We have to go now, dear," Elizabeth murmured. "They're here."

"Yes." Gracie followed her to the office, met the government officials, answered as many questions as they asked and showed them whatever they needed to see.

But her mind could not release the picture of Misty moving away from her.

If you start to worry, pray. I'll be praying for you.

"Would it be all right if we took a coffee break now?" she asked Elizabeth.

"Wonderful idea. I know our cook has prepared some delicious snacks. This way, folks."

As her boss led the licensing group toward the dining hall, Gracie locked herself in her office.

"Oh, God, please be very near my family. I love them both so much."

Family. They would be—wouldn't they?

* * *

"How are you doing?" The leader paused beside Lady, his face shiny with sweat. "I don't know where this heat is coming from." He tilted his head to the west, where clouds were galloping across the sky like a herd of wild stallions. "We'll take a break in ten minutes."

"Great. Hear that, Miss? Ten minutes and then we'll have a rest."

"I'm not tired. I love this." She certainly sounded happy. "Patch knows exactly where to go. He's the best horse."

"He sure is." Lady danced a bit and Dallas had to work to get her under control. "Come on, girl. Settle down."

"Daddy?"

He whirled in his seat at the sudden, terrified scream, saw Patch rear up. Misty grabbed his mane with both hands and bent low, her face pale. Too late Dallas saw the snake slither into the sage. Patch was off and running, so hard Misty was barely able to hang on.

"I'll get her," he yelled to the leader. "Look after the others."

Dallas knew the man couldn't leave the rest of the kids to help him. They'd need everyone to get the children back to the ranch.

Saving Misty was up to him.

"Hang on, Miss," he called, urging Lady into a full gallop. "Don't let go, baby. Keep talking to Patch while I catch him."

He reached out to grab the horse's halter, but Patch veered away, heading for a clump of mesquite. Nudging Lady's flanks, Dallas pushed her harder, came up on Misty's other side.

"Hurry, Daddy," she called. "I can't hang on."

"You have to. You're strong, Miss. Ask God to help, and don't let go."

They thundered across the dry land, farther and farther away from the group. Her horse did everything it could to escape him, but some intuition blew through Dallas's mind and told him what to do, how to move, which way to go.

Finally, with his fingers around the bridle, Dallas was able to pull on it, keeping Patch in stride with Lady as he forced both horses to slow.

"Good girl. Keep hanging on and pull on the reins, little by little. Left a bit. Good. Easy, boy. Come on. That's it, Miss. Pull him back."

Patch was clear of the mesquite, but still not at all reassured. He danced away, and Dallas lost his grip just as her mount jiggled Misty free of the saddle.

"Misty," he screamed, grabbing hold of her vest and yanking her into his arms. Startled by his sudden move, Lady shifted to accommodate his weight. But Dallas had lost his stirrups, and with both arms holding his daughter's precious weight, he couldn't keep his seat. "Hang on to me, baby. We're going to fall."

"Daddy," she squealed, her arms tight around his neck. "Help me."

"Help me."

A jumble of green brush, a small boy and his run-away dog. The memories rushed past like a video on fast-forward. The boy wasn't hurt, but he wanted his pet back, and it was headed for a very busy highway. Dallas managed to catch the puppy just before it could bound over the rail. He'd returned it to the boy, then continued his forest walk to a waterfall. But he never made it.

Three punks had dragged him off the path, beaten him unconscious.

The past events raced through his brain in a flash before Dallas saw the ground coming at him. He rolled so Misty wouldn't be crushed. Then his head hit a rock and everything went blurry.

"Daddy? Are you hurt, Daddy?"

Deep in a cavern he heard the voice, remembered his daughter.

"Why don't you talk to me, Daddy?" Small hands touched his head near the spot where pain radiated in a circle of agony. "Wake up, Daddy."

"I'm awake, Miss." Dallas lay still for a minute until the queasiness passed. Then he took stock of their surroundings. Nothing seemed familiar. He couldn't tell which direction was which. Didn't know where they should head even if he could catch the horses.

And his head hurt so badly.

"Are you injured, Miss?"

"No. I landed on you." She touched his cheek. "I think Lady ran away, Daddy."

"She'll probably go home. Horses know how to find their way home." He was going to ask her if Patch was nearby, but then remembered she wouldn't know. Wouldn't be able to see. The full impact of their situation hit him.

The leader would send someone to look for them. He'd no doubt radio in and a search party would start out immediately. But until they got here, Dallas and

Misty were in danger. The sun would quickly scorch Misty's fair skin. She'd end up with sunstroke or worse.

They had no water, no food and no shelter.

There could be snakes nearby. Or other animals.

On top of that, thunder rumbled in the distance. Judging from the threatening sky, a storm was moving their way fast.

"Listen to me, Misty. It's very important. We have to get out of the sun."

"Aren't you going to take us home?" Her voice wobbled the tiniest bit.

"As soon as I can, baby. But right now my head is bleeding. I need to rest."

"I'll look after you, Daddy. Patch!" she called, her voice softening the way he'd taught her. "Come here, Patch. Come and help Daddy."

The horse's whinny carried from some distance away. Dallas struggled to lift his head, but gagged and fought the blackness. He lay still until it receded.

"There's a stony place about twenty-five steps in front of me. It has a ledge and a scraggly tree we could sit under, where the sun wouldn't reach us. I don't feel very good so I'm counting on you to get us there. If I fall down, I want you to go to the ledge and stay there. Don't worry about me. You get there and stay. Understand?"

"Yes, Daddy. Can you walk now?"

"I don't know. Can you call Patch again?"

She did, but neither of them missed the angry bray or the thud of hooves retreating.

"Okay. Sounds like he followed Lady. It's you and I, Miss. Ready?"

"Yes." She waited till he'd dragged himself upright, then clung to his hand, stepping carefully beside him as they made their way to the ledge.

At this rate unconsciousness would return quickly. Dallas used his last ounce of strength to focus and examine the spot. No nests, no signs of animals, and best of all, no sun.

"Let's sit here, honey."

"Okay." She settled beside him, edged her way under his arm so it lay across her shoulders.

"Misty?"

"Yes, Daddy?"

"I'm not feeling too good. It might be that I'll fall asleep when you're talking to me. That's okay. You just stay put and sooner or later I'll wake up. I don't want you to leave here. Promise?"

"I promise. Are you sleepy now?"

"Sort of." He would force himself to stay conscious as long as possible, but judging by the blood soaking his hair and neck, Dallas knew that might not be for long. "I wish I'd told Gracie I loved her," he muttered.

"Mommy knows that." Misty patted his hand.

"She does?"

"Sure. People always know when other people love them. They can tell."

"How?"

"I dunno. Mommy says they just can."

He hoped she was right. He was going to need every ounce of love he could summon to gain her forgiveness. He'd promised Gracie he'd keep Misty safe. She would never trust him again.

The knowledge that God was always with him and

would never abandon him seeped into his heart. "Thank you, Father."

"What should we do, Daddy?"

"How about I tell you a story?"

"What kind of a story?" she asked, edging nearer as the thunder rumbled and the earth trembled.

"One about your mommy and me."

"Can you remember now?"

"Some things. I remember she didn't like it when I was late for stuff. She didn't say anything, but her lips would pinch together and she wouldn't look at me. I'd have to kiss her and make it better."

"What else?"

"I remember once when she fell off a bicycle. She hit a stone and boom! Over she went. She had a cut on her leg and she was almost crying."

"Did you kiss her then, too?"

"Yes." He closed his eyes, remembering the many excuses he'd found to hold Gracie, kiss her, bask in the glow she lit up inside his heart.

The memories of their courtship were precious, yet somehow new. He pulled them out one by one, savored each as he shared them with his daughter.

"I heard you talking to Mommy last night. You asked her if she wanted other kids. Do you want other kids, Daddy?"

Dallas remembered the open window and stifled a groan. He wondered how long Misty would have let the questions build if they hadn't been stuck out here. Did she think he'd love another child more than her?

"Would you like to have a brother or sister, Misty?"

"I don't know. Would you go away again?"

"No way. I'm never leaving your mom and you, Miss. I'm staying until you grow up and move away from home, and even then I'll be there. It wouldn't matter if we had ten more kids, I'd always love you because you're my beautiful daughter."

"Oh." She remained silent for several moments. "Ten kids is too many for our house, Daddy. Where would they all sleep?"

He couldn't help laughing.

The sun disappeared, the sky turned black. Apparently the weather forecasters had been wrong about the path of the storm. Rain pushed by screaming winds slashed the earth and spattered around them. Misty huddled in his arms when lightning and thunder began. But it was dry in their hiding place. It took too much effort to speak, so Dallas drew his precious daughter close as shadows lengthened and his brain grew foggy.

The last thing he heard was Misty praying.

Chapter Thirteen

"We can't send anyone after them, Gracie. The storm's made it too dangerous." Elizabeth reached out to enfold her in a comforting embrace. "No one could have known it would change direction so rapidly. But they're not alone, dear. God is with them."

"I knew something would happen."

Elizabeth didn't understand. No one did.

Gracie gave Lady another carrot. The horse had sauntered back into camp just before the storm began. She was nervous but unhurt. She was also carrying the packsack with Dallas's survival gear.

Luke had taken the horse into her stall and brushed her down. She was now happily dry.

A roar from the wranglers went up as Patch appeared. Again Luke stepped in.

All Gracie could think was that now Dallas and Misty were out there unprotected, alone.

"Go home, Gracie. Pray. As soon as the storm passes I promise I'll send someone out."

Gracie nodded, drove home in her truck. Even running the short distance from vehicle to house soaked her. She stepped into the shower, wondering how Misty and Dallas could possibly survive this torrential downpour, even if they weren't hurt.

And the lightning. She winced as another bolt appeared in the sky, stabbed the earth with a powerful flash. Smoke billowed, then disappeared as the sky went black again.

Dry and dressed in warm clothes, she switched on lights all over the house. But it still felt empty without Misty and Dallas nearby. With hot tea in hand she curled up on the love seat to watch the storm.

Dallas would protect Misty with his life. She knew that.

But what about Dallas? Who would care for him?

She picked up her Bible, but didn't know where to look, what to read. She let it fall open. Isaiah.

Wonderful, Counselor, Mighty God, Everlasting Father, Prince of Peace.

God was all of those things. He could handle a storm.

"I need him," she whispered out loud. "I need Dallas. He challenges me to live with Your tests, to face them instead of hiding, to grow and be a better mom. I need him back to help me raise Misty, to prove I won't tarnish her with my fears anymore."

Gracie padded to her bedroom, picked up the two pictures she kept on her nightstand, and carried them to the living room.

"You gave them to me," she whispered. "But not long enough. I want a chance to see Misty grow, to tell Dallas I love him. I want my family."

Gracie had been afraid to trust, because she'd

believed God was trying to punish her. For not being a better daughter, a better wife, a better mother.

With new clarity she understood that even if it hurt, God would do His very best for her. Always.

"Please stop the noise, Misty."

Only it wasn't Misty. It was the doorbell.

Gracie stumbled off the sofa, threw open the door.

A rain-soaked older couple stood on her doorstep.

"We're the Hendersons. Do you know where we can find Dallas?"

For the first time in six years Gracie felt no fear. These were not people who could ruin her. She put her faith in God's plan.

"Please come in. I'm Gracie. I married your son six years ago."

She urged them into the kitchen, put on the coffeepot as she explained what had happened. But before she could finish the story Elizabeth was tapping on her patio door.

"A search party is leaving in a few minutes. I thought you might like to go."

"I can't ride well enough," she admitted, feeling ashamed.

"You can take the all-terrain vehicle. I've put some supplies in it. Go. I'll look after things here."

"These are Dallas's parents," she said, motioning to the frightened-looking couple. "They need to know—"

"I'll take care of it. Go with God, Gracie."

Gracie was almost to the door when she caught sight of Mrs. Henderson's devastated expression.

She was a mother, too. Her only son, whom she

hadn't seen for six long years, was out there some-where. Perhaps hurt.

"Do you believe in God, Mrs. Henderson?" she asked quietly.

"Yes."

"Then depend on Him to help us find Dallas." Gracie hugged her, then walked out the door.

As she rode over the bumpy terrain behind Luke, scanning the area through binoculars, she realized the stupidity of wasting so long fearing Dallas's parents, even hating them. Their past rejection didn't matter now. Maybe Dallas's family could be hers, too, if she gave them a chance. She now believed in Dallas's promise to never take Misty from her. He wanted his family as much as she did.

They'd been searching for an hour when someone spotted Misty's bright pink barrette on the ground. From habit, Gracie thought *what if.* This time she let the thought expand.

What if they were hurt?

Then she'd find them treatment.

What if Dallas remembered?

Then they'd move on, start again.

What if the Hendersons wanted her daughter?

Then she'd teach Misty by example that love grows and expands and includes, that it never cuts anyone out of the family circle.

Life was made up of surprises. Living in fear had cost Gracie sleepless nights, precious moments in Dallas's arms. She'd almost let it cost Misty her joy in riding.

And what good had it done? Problems had come,

anyway. There were no guarantees to life. Except that God loved her husband and her child even more than she did.

And that He would give her the courage to face whatever came next.

"Over there."

She followed the riders, saw Misty seated under a ledge, smiling as if she'd just enjoyed a wonderful picnic.

Gracie scrambled out of the quad, raced across the tufts of grass and stones to collapse beside her daughter. "Misty! Are you all right?" She squeezed the precious child against her heart.

"I'm okay, Mommy. I was looking after Daddy. He's been sleeping. He was very tired. He didn't even hear all the noise in the sky. But I took care of him."

"That's wonderful, darling." Gracie looked over her shoulder, saw Dallas propped up against the rock, felt her world tilt at the sight of blood covering his clothes, the rocks, everything. "Oh, Lord, help us," she whispered.

Luke led Misty to the quad, explained that he was going to drive her back as soon as they helped her daddy. He radioed their position, and within fifteen minutes a medical chopper had landed and Dallas was being given first aid, readied for a flight to the nearest hospital.

"I'm going with him," Gracie told the attendant, but he shook his head.

"No room. We're taking him to Parkland. You'll have to get yourself there."

"I need a minute with my husband."

"Make it quick."

Gracie bent over the stretcher, brushed her hand

against his cheek. "It's me, Dallas. Gracie. It doesn't matter if you remember or not. But you made me a promise six years ago. I need you to keep that promise, Dallas. Because I love you. I love you very much. So don't even think of getting out of this marriage." She kissed him.

Within minutes he was loaded on board and the chopper had disappeared.

"Come on, Misty. We need to get you home."

"So we can go visit Daddy?"

"That and so you can meet somebody. I think you're really going to like them."

Gracie tucked her daughter into her arms and spent the ride home listening as Misty related her exciting night away from home. And as she listened, Gracie sent prayers of thanksgiving toward Heaven. God had brought them this far. Her daughter wasn't traumatized, wasn't afraid and wasn't hurt.

God wouldn't abandon them now.

It took only a few minutes for her and Misty to wash and change. Mrs. Henderson, alerted by Elizabeth, had packed a lunch, which she doled out to them as Gracie drove toward the city. With her hunger satiated, Misty closed her eyes and fell fast asleep next to the grandfather she'd just met.

"She's a wonderful child. You must be very proud," he murmured.

"Yes, I am," Gracie agreed.

"I want to apologize for our poor behavior toward you, Gracie," Mrs. Henderson stated.

"You remember?" She took her eyes from the road long enough to see regret fill the dark eyes so like Dallas's.

"Sort of. I remember you said you were married to him. We should have believed you. But we'd offered a reward for information and there were so many people claiming the same thing, and we were so distraught."

"It's not an excuse," her husband said quietly. "But we couldn't imagine that Dallas would have married without telling us. It seemed very unlikely."

"The morning after we'd sent you away, I found a note from him in the mail," Mrs. Henderson said.

Gracie's heart bumped. Answers maybe, at last? "Where was it postmarked?"

"Oregon. He told us he loved you, said that we would, too." She sniffed, wiped her eyes. "But instead of loving you, we sent you away. You were pregnant with Misty then."

"Yes."

"So you had to manage all alone. I'm so sorry." She shook her head. "We wanted to find you, but I couldn't remember your name, didn't know how to reach you. Our own foolishness made us miss knowing the best daughter and granddaughter in the world. Gracie, can you ever forgive us?"

"Of course." She felt no regret, no sadness, no anger. "It wasn't only your fault. I should have gone back to see you, persisted."

"Why didn't you?"

"I was afraid you'd try to take Misty from me. I couldn't lose her."

"Of course you couldn't. She's so precious. I just wish—"

"Let's forget the past, shall we? Let's concentrate on the present, on getting Dallas better."

"Amen," his father said from behind them.

Misty awakened when they arrived at the hospital, where they were told Dallas was in surgery. The longer it took, the more worried Gracie grew, though she tried to hide it from her child. The Hendersons took Misty to the cafeteria several times, walked outside with her, took her to the playground, anything to keep her busy.

And each time Gracie used the minutes alone to pray.

At six o'clock that evening, Dallas was rolled out of surgery and into intensive care.

"He probably won't wake up till tomorrow," the surgeon explained. "He's lost a lot of blood, but we were able to relieve the pressure on his brain. He's going to have a bad headache, but if he wakes up lucid within twenty-four hours he has a good chance of pulling through. You should try and get some rest."

"Thank you," she said quietly. "I am at rest."

"Your faith is remarkable, Gracie." Dallas's father studied her. "You don't seem at all worried. Why?"

"Credit your son. Dallas taught me to stop living in fear, to trust God to handle the parts I can't. It took me a long time to learn that lesson. He's a very special man."

"He certainly found himself a special wife."

Both parents were delighted when she suggested they visit his room first. When they emerged, white-faced but relieved, Gracie hugged them each.

"He's so pale." Mrs. Henderson seemed about to weep.

"Don't give up. God is still at work," she replied.

Gracie drew Misty into the room with her. "Daddy's asleep right now," she explained. "But I think that way deep inside he knows we're here and he can hear us. Do you want to say anything to him?"

She placed Misty's hand on Dallas's arm. Misty felt her way to his palm, tucked her fingers inside and smiled. "I could sing him my song."

"Lovely, darling. But very softly. The other patients are trying to rest."

So Misty began singing her sweet Father's Day solo to the man who'd slipped into their lives and taken over their hearts.

"Your daddy must be very proud of you," one of the nurses said.

"He loves me," Misty told her. "And I love him. When he wakes up we're going on another horse ride."

It was late when they left Dallas's room. Misty was visibly drooping.

"There's a very nice hotel nearby. Why don't we all go and rest for a while?" Mrs. Henderson urged, scooping the little girl into her arms. Misty laid her head on the comfortable shoulder and promptly fell asleep.

"I want to stay with Dallas," Gracie told them. She whispered a prayer, then took another step of faith. "Would it be too much to ask you to look after Misty tonight? She's very tired. I'm pretty sure she won't wake up during the night, but if she does, you could call me here and I'd come immediately."

"We'd be honored, Gracie," Mr. Henderson declared. "Thank you for trusting us."

She did trust them, which was a wonderful feeling. But she also trusted God. When they left, Gracie returned to Dallas's bedside, linked her fingers with his and sat down to wait for him to waken.

And while she waited, she talked to the One who held the world in His hands.

Chapter Fourteen

Dallas lay perfectly still, waiting for the blackness to overtake his mind again.

When nothing happened he opened his eyes, saw a familiar sun-streaked head lying by his hand.

Gracie.

He knew her.

He knew the way she'd awaken, pulling out of sleep in slow motion. He knew the way her mouth would curve, how her blue eyes would wrinkle at the edges when she smiled. He knew her voice would resemble rough velvet when she spoke the first words of the day. He knew a thousand other details that had lain hidden for so long.

Thank You, God.

"Wake up, sleepyhead," he murmured, touching her cheek with the tips of his fingers, so she wouldn't startle.

She uncurled from her slumber like a cat, blinked her incredible lashes, smiled and sent his heart monitor into overdrive.

"You're awake," she whispered.

"So are you."

A nurse came in, adjusted the machine and grinned. "Take it easy, okay?"

Dallas smiled back, then remembered.

"Misty?" He jerked upright, winced at the stabbing pain. A quick glance didn't locate her blond curls nearby. "Is she hurt?"

"Misty's fine, Dallas. She's with your parents at a hotel."

"Mom and Dad arrived? You met them?" Her nod released a stress he hadn't known he felt. "Great. You'll love them."

"Misty said you remembered everything."

"Not everything, but most of it. I got mugged, Gracie, jumped and beaten when I was scouting some land."

"Why would you be scouting land? For work?"

He shook his head, unable to tear his gaze from her beloved face. "I'm not a complete loser, Gracie. I didn't walk away without a plan for our future. I just wanted to keep it all a secret until I could surprise you. Dumb idea."

"Yes, it was," she agreed tartly. "So what's the surprise?"

"It's probably gone by now, not that we need it. But I found this piece of land. I was eating in the airport in Vancouver and I heard these two men talking about a huge piece of estate property that was being subdivided in the hills outside L.A. I decided to check it out. It was kind of in a forest."

"This can wait, Dallas."

"No, I want to tell you. There was this kid, and his dog got away, so I had to rescue it. Regret," he said, suddenly remembering. "The dog's name was Regret. That's why I kept seeing the word."

Gracie lifted an eyebrow. "You're going to tell me the dog mugged you?"

"No, silly." He pulled her close, kissed her as he'd longed to, the way he kissed her when they'd been apart too long and he hadn't seen her for a while. "I love you. Do you know that? I was going to tell you before I went on that ride, but I thought I'd wait, let you see that your fears were groundless, that God was in control."

The enormity of what had happened hit home like a sledgehammer. The worry he'd put Gracie through—it was unimaginable.

"I was wrong. I shouldn't have taken Misty."

"Are you kidding me?" Gracie pushed him back so that his head rested on the pillow. "I'm sorry you got hurt, Dallas. But that ride, looking after you—Misty has a confidence she would never have gained otherwise." Tears washed the blue to silver, but they were not sad tears.

He caught one on his finger, marveling at the change a day made, to all of them.

"You kept your promise, Dallas. And God kept His. Misty came shining through."

He couldn't find any fear in her eyes.

"I love you, Gracie Henderson," he breathed. "I've missed you, wife."

"I missed you, too, husband." She kissed him, then drew away, her face bright pink. "People are staring at us."

"Who cares?" But he contented himself with holding her hand. "I want to go home and be with my family. When can I get out of here?"

"When the doctors say and not a moment sooner. We're not taking any chances, Dallas."

"Chances on what? I'm fine. I know what I want. And it's all on the Bar None."

"You might be going somewhere else."

Gracie had turned a very interesting shade of red and she wouldn't look at him.

"I might? Where?"

"Elizabeth told me she thinks we should take some time off. Together."

"I always said Elizabeth is a very smart woman." Dallas kissed Gracie's lips, then winked at the old man in the next bed. "I've been away for a while," he said.

"How long?"

"Six years."

"Man, are you going to be busy. You owe her some serious makeup time."

"Fine by me." Dallas saw Misty and his parents waiting outside the door.

"I'm going to tell the office to move you out of here," the nurse said with a smile. "This place is for sick people."

So they took turns with him. First his mom and dad. He caught up with them, learned they had completed a tour of missions in Bali and had decided to visit Australia before they returned to Dallas.

"We thought about keeping the house, but when you didn't come back, we decided it was better to get on with life."

"You were right, Dad. I wouldn't have wanted you to stay. You always talked about going to see the mission you supported for so long," Dallas mused. "I'm glad you finally went."

"It was fun. But we won't be going back," his mother informed him. "Not now that we've got a daughter-in-law and a granddaughter to spoil. But I'm quite upset with you. How could you not invite us to the wedding?"

"I would have, if you two hadn't been off gallivanting halfway 'round the world."

"I assure you, son," his father grumbled, "we're not leaving Texas for the foreseeable future. Who knows what you might do next."

"Is it ever going to be my turn to talk to my daddy?" Misty asked from the doorway.

His parents shared a grin.

"She reminds me a lot of you," his mother murmured. "And it's not just the dimples. Come on in, Misty. It's your turn. Grandpa and I have some things to do." She hugged Dallas close, then drew away, her eyes watery. "We love you."

"I love you, too. Can you call me later this afternoon, Mom? I need to ask you to do something."

They left and Gracie came in, but she and Misty were only there for a few minutes before the doctor arrived.

"I'm going home for a shower and to check on things. I'll be back later," Gracie promised, squeezing his hand. "Do exactly what they say. I don't want any relapses."

He drew her down, kissed her with his heart and soul.

"Is that the kiss of a man who's going to have a relapse?" he demanded.

"See what I mean, Doctor?" The nurse winked at him. Gracie scurried away, but she didn't look upset.

Dallas turned to the doctor. "Okay, Doc. Let's talk about getting me out of here."

In the end, it took four long days for Dallas's release.

Four days of stolen kisses and whispers of love. Four days of secret plans and a lot of prayer. Four days of wonderful laughter and murmured promises.

And Dallas loved every moment.

Chapter Fifteen

He's coming home. He's coming home.

The refrain spun around and around in Gracie's head.

She pulled into the hospital parking lot, and her heart hit overdrive when she saw Dallas lounging on the bench outside the main door.

"You were supposed to wait inside," she scolded. "Don't they wheel you out in a chair or something when you're released?"

"Not to worry," he said, right before he kissed her.

It was ridiculous the way her knees went weak every time he was near. No matter how many times he embraced her, each was new and wonderful.

"The van's over there."

"Can we walk in the garden first?"

Sensing Dallas had something he needed to say, she nodded, let him lead her to an uninhabited spot, and sat down on the bench there. To her amazement, he knelt in front of her.

"Gracie Henderson, will you marry me?"

She giggled. "I'm already married to you. Did you forget again?"

"No. Will you marry me, please? Again?"

The seriousness in his eyes, the yearning in his voice compelled her to answer. "Anytime, anyplace," she whispered.

"How about today?"

He held out a small black box. Gracie flipped open the lid. She gasped at the beautiful diamond solitaire perched on a bed of black velvet, was too shocked to speak as he slid the ring onto her finger.

"It's going to be a short engagement," he warned.

She tore her eyes from the stone, frowned at him. "What do you mean?"

"The ceremony is scheduled for this afternoon." He slid his hands to her face, pressed a delicate butterfly kiss to each eye. "Is it a deal, darling Gracie?"

"I can't get married in this." She gestured to her worn jeans and tired sweater.

"No, you certainly can't." Dallas's mother surged toward them. "We have a lot of things to do. Kiss your bride and let us get to it."

"Yes, Mother." Dallas drew Gracie to her feet, wrapped his arms around her and held her against his heart. "Trust me, darling?"

"Always."

Excitement built as she waved goodbye before following her mother-in-law to a waiting limo. "Where are we going?"

"Hair salon. Then to pick up your dress."

"My dress." Bemusement blurred everything. "What's it like?"

"You'll have to wait and see."

"Misty. What about Misty? She should be a part of this."

"Oh, she is. She and Elizabeth are tending to other details. As a good bridesmaid and a flower girl should."

"Dallas arranged all this?"

"Well, he had a little help." Mrs. Henderson preened.

They both laughed. Gracie leaned back against the smooth leather seat, prepared to relax and enjoy. She had her hair cut and styled, then a manicure and a pedicure, with Misty for company. After a short stop for some iced tea it was off to the bridal shop.

"Hold up your arms and close your eyes, dear. Hester, I don't want her hair mussed."

"Yes, Mrs. Henderson," the bridal shop owner murmured.

With a whoosh a silken garment slid down Gracie's arms. Behind her someone fastened a zipper.

"Okay. You can look."

It was a ballerina dress. The bodice was fitted with the daintiest of straps and cinched in around her waist. Below that the tulle skirt billowed out, layer upon layer of the most delicate fabric Gracie had ever seen, tumbling down to her pink-tinted toenails.

"Slip these on, honey."

Gracie slid her feet into white sandals that looked lethal but were so comfortable.

"Dallas chose your dress."

Then she remembered. He'd talked about just such a dress the day she'd found him, when she'd told him about their first wedding.

"It's the most beautiful dress I've ever seen."

"It's you who is beautiful, dear. I've never seen a lovelier bride."

"What about me? What do I wear?" Misty demanded. "Hester?"

Misty's dress was almost an exact match to Gracie's, except the child's was in the palest of pale yellows, repeated in the rosebuds tucked into her silver-gold curls. She had short white socks and white patent shoes that tapped when she walked.

"Am I pretty, Mommy?"

"You're so lovely I can hardly believe you're my daughter."

"Well, I am. But I wish I didn't have to wear these socks. I want Daddy to see my painted toenails. I never had painted toenails before, did I?"

"You can take your shoes off later, honey," Mrs. Henderson told her. "But right now we've got to get going. Dallas was very specific about the time the ceremony would take place."

The same time as the last one. Gracie smiled. He'd planned all of this to give them a new start, a new memory. A new beginning.

Their family, starting off whole and strong and together.

Her heart ached with love for this wonderful man.

"I have to make one stop," she told Mrs. Henderson. "The jewelers. I want to buy a new wedding ring for Dallas. He told me the muggers stole his."

"I thought you might feel that way. Will this do?" Mrs. Henderson set a wide band of platinum on her palm. "I told Dallas's jeweler it should match yours."

"Thank you," Gracie said, hugging her. How could she ever have feared this woman would be an enemy?

"Don't thank me. I haven't had this much fun in years. The bouquets are in the car. Let's go."

Gracie could hardly endure the ride to the arboretum. She needed to see Dallas, needed to thread her hand in his, watch his eyes sparkle when he saw Misty. She needed to hear him say he loved her.

She needed to tell him the same thing.

"Here we are."

Once they were out of the car, Elizabeth joined them.

"You look very beautiful, Gracie. Is it all right for me to be your bridesmaid?"

"Who else? You're the one who brought us together again. I'm honored, Elizabeth."

In the distance Pastor Mike stood waiting. Dallas stood with his back to her, talking to his father, who touched his arm. Her husband turned, and as their eyes met, Gracie felt the same burst of joy she'd experienced six years ago. He was wearing a white shirt, black pants, and of course, his boots. His white Stetson gleamed in the sunshine.

"I'm ready," she whispered.

"All right then. Misty, remember what we practiced?"

"Twenty-five steps. Where's my basket?"

"Right here." Music floated across the grass on a gentle breeze. "Off you go now."

Misty walked across the grass slowly, with great aplomb, dropping tiny yellow rose petals in front of her to create a path. Gracie noticed several bystanders turn to watch. No wonder. Her daughter was a special gift from God. One of many.

Misty reached her twenty-fifth step, moved to the left.

"Now you, Elizabeth. Here are your flowers."

"Thank you." Elizabeth followed Misty's path.

"Gracie, these are from Dallas. With love."

She stared at the sheaf of golden roses. The yellow rose of Texas. Dallas had sung that song to her often six years ago, strumming his guitar like a proud cowboy.

Her cowboy.

"Are you ready, dear?"

"Yes."

And she was. Ready to embrace everything God had in store for her.

Gracie walked down the rose petal aisle with her eyes firmly fixed on Dallas. She put her hand in his, repeated the vows she'd made six years ago, and received his promise in return.

"I now pronounce you man and wife. You may kiss your bride."

And he did.

"Aren't they ever going to stop, Granny? I want to show Daddy my toes."

Gracie felt Dallas's shoulders shake.

"That's our daughter."

The afternoon flew past. Mrs. Henderson had thought of everything. A photographer snapped a thousand pictures, a caterer served a wonderful buffet to friends and family, while a trio of guitarists serenaded anyone who cared to listen.

When she finally got a moment alone with Dallas, Gracie led him to the edge of the lake that bordered the arboretum. "I need to talk to you about something."

He leaned against a tree, drew her close. "Is it important?"

"Yes. You once asked me where I saw myself in ten years."

He said nothing, eyes glowing, as he waited.

"I see myself with you, Dallas. Loving you."

"And where do you see all this happening, my darling Gracie?"

"That's what we need to discuss. Yesterday Elizabeth offered me a permanent position at the Bar None. She's going to ask you to stay, too, to organize a research project into the relationship between disabled children and the use of animals in their therapies. I said I had to talk to you before I could give her an answer."

"I see."

"Where do you want to live, Dallas? Place isn't important to me. I'll be happy anywhere, as long as you're there. So you choose."

"I can't." He kissed her nose. "This is a family. Everyone gets a vote. I suggest we ask Misty."

"I want to stay at the ranch, Daddy," Misty said. "Rory's going to be my boyfriend and we're going to go riding again."

Gracie hadn't even heard her daughter approach. But as she watched Dallas, saw his eyes crinkle with joy, she knew Misty's choice was the right one.

"I'd like to stay, too, Miss. I can hardly wait to get started on my research, though I'm going to miss being Mommy's helper."

"You can still be her helper." Misty flopped down on the ground, pulled off her shoes and socks and held up her feet for his inspection. "A lady put stuff on them just like Mommy's."

"Very nice." He tickled her toes until she wiggled

away, doubled over with giggles. "How can I be Mommy's helper, honey?"

"You can help her find me a sister. We got a granny and a grandpa, a daddy and a mommy and me. But families can grow, can't they, Daddy?"

"Yes, my darling. Families can grow and grow. Right, wife?" He tossed his Stetson in the air, then lifted Gracie into his arms and swung her around.

"Very right, husband," she agreed, hanging on. "I guess you get to be a real cowboy, after all."

"Being your cowboy will always be my highest honor."

And he sealed his promise with a kiss.

* * * * *

Hello again!

I'm so glad you could join me for this final installment in the PENNIES FROM HEAVEN series. In some ways the last book in a series is always the hardest to let go because you've fallen in love with your characters. That's certainly true with Dallas and Gracie. They started off with such high dreams and sank to the pit of despair before finding each other again.

Gracie had six years to stew and fuss and worry. Though depending on God was always her best choice, she had to make the decision and stick with it in spite of her worst fears. Dallas wanted to honor the commitment he made, but with no past to guide him, he had to hang tight to his faith. What God really wants is for us to be like Misty, blind to everything but the path He leads us on.

I would love to hear from you. Write to me at loisricher@yahoo.com or via snail mail at Box 639, Nipawin, Saskatchewan, Canada S0E 1E0. You can check me out on the Web at www.loisricher.com.

Till we meet again I wish you God's richest joy, His deepest peace and His unfaltering love.

Blessings,

Lois Richer

QUESTIONS FOR DISCUSSION

1. Discuss a time when your deepest hopes and dreams were crushed. What was your response? Did you think this was God's punishment? How did you move on?

2. Many people believe being a Christian means a guaranteed life of ease. List Scriptures that disprove this theory. Besides Heaven, what does being a Christian guarantee?

3. In the story, Misty was born blind. This presented a new set of problems for her mother, but made Misty more attuned to her other senses. Because she'd never known anything else, Misty maximized her sensory abilities. Suggest ways personalities have an impact on our responses to others. Are there ways we can enhance our natural God-given abilities to improve the way we see, hear or touch the lives of others?

4. Elizabeth Wisdom took great care that the Bar None boasted the latest equipment and most highly trained employees to maximize the children's results. Discuss the impact charities have in your communities and ways you can assist them in helping others.

5. Dallas struggled to understand some past choices he'd made. Share ways to ensure our decisions are made for the right reasons.

6. Most people have issues that push their hot buttons and add worry and concern. Are there ways to diminish these effects? Discuss practical solutions for cracking the cycle of fear.

7. Gracie discovered that her daughter was picking up on her personal problems even though Gracie tried to hide them. Children are particularly susceptible to their parents' beliefs, actions and doubts. How does this impact the parental role? What positive things can children adopt from their parents?

8. Because of one very negative interaction with Dallas's parents, Gracie built up a problem that loomed large in her life. Share events that you over-magnified. Did any later turn out to be blessings? How so?

9. When is fear beneficial to a Christian? What impact have your fears had on you? What role has your faith played in overcoming your fears?

10. The nuclear family is shrinking in society. List ways we can protect our families so that our beliefs and ethics are passed on.

REQUEST YOUR FREE BOOKS!

2 FREE INSPIRATIONAL NOVELS
PLUS 2
FREE
MYSTERY GIFTS

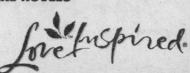

YES! Please send me 2 FREE Love Inspired® novels and my 2 FREE mystery gifts (gifts are worth about $10). After receiving them, if I don't wish to receive any more books, I can return the shipping statement marked "cancel". If I don't cancel, I will receive 4 brand-new novels every month and be billed just $4.24 per book in the U.S. or $4.74 per book in Canada, plus 25¢ shipping and handling per book and applicable taxes, if any*. That's a savings of over 20% off the cover price! I understand that accepting the 2 free books and gifts places me under no obligation to buy anything. I can always return a shipment and cancel at any time. Even if I never buy another book, the two free books and gifts are mine to keep forever.

113 IDN ERXA 313 IDN ERWX

Name	(PLEASE PRINT)

Address	Apt. #

City	State/Prov.	Zip/Postal Code

Signature (if under 18, a parent or guardian must sign)

Order online at www.LoveInspiredBooks.com
Or mail to Steeple Hill Reader Service:
IN U.S.A.: P.O. Box 1867, Buffalo, NY 14240-1867
IN CANADA: P.O. Box 609, Fort Erie, Ontario L2A 5X3
Not valid to current subscribers of Love Inspired books.

Want to try two free books from another series?
Call 1-800-873-8635 or visit www.morefreebooks.com

* Terms and prices subject to change without notice. N.Y. residents add applicable sales tax. Canadian residents will be charged applicable provincial taxes and GST. This offer is limited to one order per household. All orders subject to approval. Credit or debit balances in a customer's account(s) may be offset by any other outstanding balance owed by or to the customer. Please allow 4 to 6 weeks for delivery. Offer available while quantities last.

Your Privacy: Steeple Hill Books is committed to protecting your privacy. Our Privacy Policy is available online at www.SteepleHill.com or upon request from the Reader Service. From time to time we make our lists of customers available to reputable third parties who may have a product or service of interest to you. If you would prefer we not share your name and address, please check here. ☐

LIREG0‍

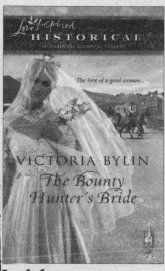

TITLES AVAILABLE NEXT MONTH

Don't miss these four stories in May

TO LOVE AGAIN by Bonnie K. Winn
A Rosewood, Texas novel

Laura Manning moved her family to Rosewood to take over her
late husband's share of a real-estate firm. Who was Paul Russell to
tell her she couldn't? She'd prove to the handsome Texan that she
could do anything.

A SOLDIER'S HEART by Marta Perry
The Flanagans

After wounded army officer Luke Marino was sent home, he
refused physical therapy. But Mary Kate Flanagan Donnelly
needed Luke's case to prove herself a capable therapist. If only
it wasn't so hard to keep matters strictly business...

MOM IN THE MIDDLE by Mae Nunn
Texas Treasures

Juggling caring for her son and elderly parents kept widow
Abby Cramer busy. Then her mother broke her hip at a store.
Good thing store employee Guy Hardy rushed in to save the day
with his tender kindness toward her whole family—especially
Abby herself.

HOME SWEET TEXAS by Sharon Gillenwater
When a strange man appeared to her like a mirage in the desert,
he was the answer to the lost and injured woman's prayers. But
she couldn't tell her handsome rescuer, Jake Trayner, who she
was. Because she couldn't remember....

LICNM040